The Gift

that is

Ruby's Place

Holly Schindler

Schindler

The Gift That Is Ruby's Place

Published by InToto Books

Copyright © 2020 by Holly Schindler

Formatted and designed by Holly Schindler

Images by Alexander Raths, Aleksandrs Bondars, and Piotr Krzeslak, all courtesy of Shutterstock

Fonts: Columbia by ultra letter, hey butterfly by NJ Studio, and My Skinny Type by Joanne's Letters, all courtesy of Font Bundles

"When I was younger, I could remember anything, whether it happened or not —"

Mark Twain

Author's Note

There's just something about a bar in winter. It has a certain romantic charm. Night falls early, letting the stars pop against the sky as you hurry down the sidewalk, toward your favorite gathering place. It's cold, so you huddle close to your loved one—maybe you grasp each other's hands, or he puts an arm around your shoulder. Your breath comes in quick white puffs, because you're laughing.

Inside, the bar is warm and full of voices. You are welcomed by familiar faces and a kind of fiery yellow glow. You hang your coats by the door. With the holidays on the horizon, everything tastes sweeter, even your favorite cocktail, the one you always order.

You feel as though you're all huddling together, hiding from the outdoor cold. Your love blows on your fingers to warm them up. Candles glow on tables. You are sitting next to a window, and when it starts to snow, it looks like a postcard. Or maybe that's a Christmas card, inscribed with wishes for the season.

Yes, there's just something about a bar in the winter.

But there's also something about a favorite bar, a corner bar, the bar you have always visited. It has a certain comfort. A rhythm. A friendly predictability in knowing you have a seat waiting for you, that you will catch up with the same faces and hear many of the same wild stories and jokes.

Rarely do these establishments ever find themselves the subject of any kind of front-page headline, any special interest news stories. They simply are. We trick ourselves into thinking they will always be.

A few years ago, when my city was debating a ban on smoking in public areas, one of those small corner bars did find itself on the news. The owner indicated the ban would cut into her business dangerously, possibly forcing her to close.

There was just something about the sight of that owner, her face a hazy image in the front window as she looked out. Something about her insistence that the one thing she knew how to do well was run her bar…

It stuck with me.

I started thinking about a story of a fictional bar owner. One who was similarly good at running a bar—so good, in fact, that she was still there, running that bar after her own death.

Yes, there was just something about that face—something about Christmas—something about a winter night at a bar—that inspired me to get to the keyboard.

I've been writing installments about Ruby's Place since 2017. This year's finale is actually written as a standalone, so even if you haven't read another installment, you'll be able to jump right in. If you've been reading all along, you'll see previous events from a brand-new angle, learn new previously undisclosed truths about the main characters. It's been an utter delight, each year, to travel to my fictional town of Sullivan and open the bright green entrance of my imagined corner bar.

I hope you'll agree there's also something about Ruby's Place. And I thank you for taking the journey with me.

Holly Schindler

The Bottom Drawer

In Sullivan, a small Missouri town, the history museum preserves what otherwise might be lost forever.

Towns like Sullivan are usually shunted to footnotes. The entire town. What happened there, most of the history books insist, spurred no important movements, shaped no groundbreaking world events.

It is up to the people of the town to make sure their stories endure.

Wills in Sullivan, therefore, direct cardboard boxes or trunks or even safe deposit boxes be bequeathed to Toby, the museum director. Contents include pictures. Sometimes, over the years, he's gotten cassette tapes. Oral stories. Handwritten letters.

Don't forget, the treasures all implore.

Toby documents everything, dutifully. At times, the newest donations inspire exhibits, to be shown to the public by Linda Bryant, Sullivan's retired high school Latin teacher.

"If you can get seventeen-year-olds excited about conjugating verbs, you can get visitors excited about the past,"

Toby tells her often.

But in truth, it takes no work to excite them. The past belongs to them, their families, their ancestors—and that in itself makes it interesting. Combined, it creates a road map that shows all the journeys that had to take place for each one of them to even exist.

Sullivan is, it often seems, a town built out of memories.

Toby's storage methods are the meticulous ways of any historian—acid-free papers and climate control. Always gloves when handling the most fragile items.

He has separate cabinets and folders for blueprints and building specs and legal filings. Stories are arranged by decade, then broken down again alphabetically by families' last names.

No single entry takes up much space…

Except for Ruby's Place.

The old bar, situated on the town square, has provided the source of more interest and donations than any single place or event or person ever to cross or take place or dwell within the city limits. So many, they fill an entire cabinet all on their own.

Toby has preserved old local newspaper stories and pictures of the place, some of which have faded enough that he has hired photograph restorers. A few diaries. Occasionally, cocktail recipes or a small Christmas decoration. An original song, in one instance. A trumpet's mouthpiece, in another. An old candlestick phone once used inside the bar.

"It's important," he's been told. "You can't ever throw

this away. "

So he hasn't—none of it. Over the past few years, patterns have slowly begun to emerge. Stories have started overlapping.

And still, he has discarded nothing. Even when a donation tells a story he has already preserved. Each new item offers documentation from a new perspective. He places the most interesting pieces in the bottom drawer of the Ruby's Place cabinet. Those items have, over the years, begun to talk, relating their role in Ruby's long and varied chapters. Or so Toby thinks.

Toby himself is getting on in years—he often jokes he has yellowed around the edges himself. Gotten crinkly and faded, just like the donations that come his way. Maybe, he sometimes thinks, a person gets a bit more sentimental in their advanced years. Maybe you are just as apt to believe in the unfathomable or the magical as you once were as a child.

Regardless, those items in the bottom drawer of the Ruby's Place cabinet all paint a picture. Something truly special happens inside that old bar.

Especially during the holidays.

That's why the label Toby has placed on that bottom drawer reads, simply, "December."

Geena
Last Year

I guess you could say it all started on Christmas Eve.

The kind of magical, sparkling Christmas Eve that you assume, at a certain age, will never come back around again. A Christmas when nothing looks plastic or fake or made up. A Christmas during which the stars feel like they're not just shining for you, they *see* you. They know exactly what you want. A Christmas that lets you believe, with your entire heart, in the idea that the world really is a place where if you dream hard enough, and you really are good enough, even your most unrealistic, pie-in-the-sky wish can be granted.

Rather than finding myself seated beside a roaring fire, admiring a beautifully decorated tree and piles of brightly wrapped gifts, I was carrying a tray, passing out cocktail glasses, making sure I left one for myself. Excitement tingled against my skin like falling snowflakes. It was the second Christmas Eve for the reopened Ruby's Place, a bar on the square of Sullivan, Missouri. The second Christmas Eve I'd volunteered to work, helping out the new owner.

It was still early in the evening—so early, the "Closed" sign was still turned toward the sidewalk. Right then, the bar was empty except for the owner, Angela, and my Rob, and a small group of friends gearing up for the night's festivities. We might've called ourselves waitstaff if we were there for money and not there as a favor to Angela. The scent of pine filled the air. Red and green napkins and polished silverware added a festive touch to the white tablecloths. The piano was tinkling a warm-up. Maddie, a sweet little nine-year-old in a plaid dress with a velvet collar, was swinging her legs from the piano bench as she stuck out her tongue and struck an awkward chord. Candles were being lit on each table as she launched into her first public performance of "Jingle Bells," the learning of which had been a present for her mother. And why *wouldn't* the piano in Ruby's be perfect for the giving of such a gift? It didn't matter that neither Maddie nor her mother had ever stepped inside Ruby's before that night. In the way of small towns, they were as welcome to that piano as the oldest of friends.

Maybe, I was thinking, we could make this good-luck toast before officially unlocking the door to Christmas Eve revelers our ritual. The holidays were full of them—rituals, traditions, things we did every single year, no questions asked, often *just because*. Me, I'd been coming back to my childhood hometown every holiday season of my adult life. Back to re-assuringly familiar streets, to the same vintage silver stars decorating the streetlights along the town's main thoroughfares, and to the comfortable house where I had been a girl. Those days, I was also returning to my first and best love. My Rob.

That night, his was the glass I most wanted to clink against my own.

It was a *to us* as much as a *to another successful night at Ruby's* when we toasted. He winked at me in the moment before I placed my own glass to my lips. And with that wink, it hit, like a ritual in itself—that loop-the-loop drop in my stomach because Rob was there, he was with me.

I was expecting to taste a perfectly pleasant, warm, wintry cocktail. One of Angela's newest concoctions. But what hit my tongue when I knocked the glass back was the worst tasting excuse for a drink I'd ever had—like gasoline and herbs and dust, with a dash of pure fire added in for good measure. Before I could so much as cough, I saw a flash of light. Which terrified me, if you want to know the truth. Wasn't that the old story about moonshine? That drinking the vile stuff could actually make a person go blind? Had Angela gotten her hands on some sort of local booze-gone-wrong?

"Geena?" Rob asked. "Gene? You okay?"

I blinked away the white burst, only to find Rob's sweet, handsome face hovering in front of mine. Not the middle-aged face I had reunited with, though—I was staring at a sixteen-year-old Rob, the boy with the long hair and mischievous eyes. It was the face he'd worn when he still had that stolen shot glass tied to the rearview mirror of his Caprice with a scrunchie. *Toxic*, that was the word that had trailed after him back then—and that had been lobbed at me as a warning. *That guy's too wild for you.* It was the same face that had once made me—bookish Geena Barister with the glasses and the straight-As—feel alive and reckless and free.

"Geena?" he asked again.

Blinking again, I was once more staring into Rob's forty-eight-year-old face. The one with the crinkles spilling out from the corners of his eyes and the short hair that had gone gray at the temples. Something else had happened when I'd gulped that cocktail. It had left me with a funny feeling. Hadn't I realized something? Something about Ruby's, maybe?

Whatever it had been slipped away from me, like a dream that instantly grew hazy upon waking. All that remained was the fact that I'd just seen Rob's younger face.

"Did you just—" he started, gesturing toward his own glass.

"This stuff is awful," I said, quickly dismissing what I'd seen. Mostly because it didn't seem entirely merry. And all I really wanted to do was revel in the Christmas feeling.

We laughed as we made faces, grimacing at the taste of the cocktails. It's the way of a real love, though, isn't it? The most cringeworthy things can become jokes.

Angela slipped out from behind the bar, crossed her fingers, and flipped the "Open" sign toward the sidewalk. The bright green door swiveled, allowing the bar to quickly fill with a burst of happy chatter. The entire line that had stretched down the street, all the merrymakers who'd flocked to Ruby's Place for Christmas Eve, began flowing inside.

I watched as friendly faces chose tables or paused to chat. In the tiny town of Sullivan, Ruby's Place was *it*, where everyone wanted to be seen. Not a single place could compare. The lovely little bar behind the red neon Ruby's sign defied the very definition of "bar," with its linen tablecloths and crystal chandeliers and live music and an unusual menu that included fresh cocoa with homemade marshmallows. "Supper club," that was the term Ruby herself had used when she'd owned the place. And every single person in Sullivan was a member. Everyone was received with open arms—even the kids. They raced to celebrate in their finest attire, with their finest kindnesses on display.

All around me, the joyous festivity rolled on. Shouting and singing and waves of laughter made it hard for me to take orders. Angela shared her homemade marshmallows with Maddie, who giggled as she smeared the sticky sweets everywhere. Shiny gift wrappings were shredded from boxes and began to litter the floor. I ducked as kisses were blown and received with warm smiles. Promises were made that this next year would be even better. One for the record books. *I love you*s were exchanged. I sat customers and took coats and delivered drinks, weaving in and out of the crowd.

Hours later, as the place finally quieted down, I grabbed my own coat and headed outside for a deep breath or two. It was after midnight, so I guess technically it was Christmas Day. It certainly felt like the thick of night, though, with the stars overhead and the red neon blazing over Ruby's door.

Rob was still inside the bar, helping Angela with the last few cleanup details. Dishes were done, the floor mopped, every last candle extinguished. I could see him through the front window, and caught myself thinking of him yet again as my boyfriend. Such a juvenile term, really: *boyfriend.* The kind that, more than halfway through my forties, made me grit my teeth. I hadn't always felt that way, though. All I had to do to remember a time I'd felt entirely different was look down at the sidewalk beneath my feet, at the message that had been carved into the cement back when it had just been poured:

Rob & Geena 4Ever 1987.

Back then, *boyfriend* had seemed pretty darned grown-up. Standing there, more than thirty years after Rob had carved our names and a full year after Rob and I had found each other again, I felt myself overwhelmed by the same rush of emotions I usually got watching old home movies or hearing a song from my high school days on the radio. Kind of this painful twinge of nostalgia. What was it about looking back that made you feel that way? It was a pleasurable kind of hurt, like a loose tooth you couldn't keep your hands off of.

For the first time that night, though, I kind of felt a little sour, too. And I wondered if I wasn't just missing who I'd been back then, the Geena of *Rob & Geena 4Ever 1987.* The girl who'd believed that she could do anything—for me, that was write. Write something big, something important, something memorable. There it was again, the old dream: to become one of the greats whose short stories or novels were anthologized in textbooks.

But the writing had never happened. I was Dr. Barister, professor of American literature. As for Rob, by then, he owned The Page Turner new and used books, just across the street from Ruby's Place. A business that, despite his best efforts, was absolutely floundering. He didn't think I knew, but

I did. He was struggling to keep the lights on.

That much hadn't exactly been part of his youthful dreams, either.

The square was eerily quiet. The kind of quiet that meant your mind could quickly switch from one thought to another—heading through all the darker places the outside world was usually so good at distracting you from. Suddenly, the sourness was clouding the sweetness of the evening. My thoughts were careening toward my dad being gone. He'd died the year before, a heart attack right there on the square, and it was still hard for me to wrap my mind around the fact that I wasn't going to see him that Christmas season, or any other, not ever again.

I was shivering—more from my thoughts than the December cold. No matter where I looked, Rob's store was visible in my peripheral vision, his dreams for the future glowing in the nearby streetlight and teetering on the brink all at the same time. And no matter which direction my thoughts turned, I could also feel, in my heart's peripheral vision, the fact that I had not published the Great American Novel. I hadn't even written sentence one.

I was so far away from that girl who had first laid eyes on Rob's sixteen-year-old face. The strange way his young face had flashed in front of me earlier that night only drove home all the time that had passed. Suddenly, in my head, I was cataloging all the things I'd done. All the things I had not done.

Maybe, if I were to be honest, what was really bugging me right then, more than anything, was that my excuses for not writing were falling apart. My teaching contract was up for renewal at the university in Iowa, but right there in Missouri, I had inherited my childhood home. Owned it outright. And I had money in the bank. Not a lot, but enough to keep me for a year if I watched it.

I officially had what I'd spent my entire adult life grumbling that I didn't have: an opportunity. I could decline the contract renewal, stay at home, and write. A year was surely enough to get it done. And then, if it turned out to be as good as I'd always imagined it'd be, I'd have the kind of cash that could help Rob.

And yet...

Write about *what*? And *how*? I'd had ideas, sure. Hundreds of them. Ideas that had come and gone. Seemed silly. Or dull. Done a million times before. Right then, I felt tapped. I had no current outlines, no general direction, not a single storyline to plot. Not even the vaguest clue how to begin. After so many years of studying and critiquing others' literary works, when it came to putting my own backside in a chair to begin my own masterpiece—I was lost.

It was a crummy feeling, the suspicion that maybe, you weren't really as good as you'd once believed.

Really, it felt like it was midnight in so many ways. Like it was maybe midnight inside me.

But then I noticed it. Poking out of a snowdrift beside the door of Ruby's.

A bottle.

On impulse, I tugged at it, freeing it from the white mound of snow supporting it.

The bottle was old. With a cork and a faded paper

label that was loose at the sides and about to fall off. Initially, I thought it might be an old wine bottle, saved because the evening had been someone's special occasion. A life-changing night. Maybe a couple who had gotten engaged over two glasses of the stuff (and somebody was always getting engaged on Christmas Eve at Ruby's Place) had asked Angela if they could keep the bottle for luck—and dropped it by accident in their hurry to get home.

But it wasn't shaped like a wine bottle. On the label, I could faintly make out the word "rum." I remembered Angela saying something recently about rum being the favorite of the bar's original owner, the actual Ruby of Ruby's Place. Not that I was all that sure how it played into this particular find. After all, Ruby had passed away ages ago—while I was still working on my bachelor's, it seemed. I shook it, finding a bit of liquid still inside. And when I held it closer to the streetlight, it appeared someone had shoved a bough of mistletoe inside.

"I do believe you've had a bit too much Christmas, old girl," I scolded myself. Who put mistletoe in rum? Probably herbs of some kind.

I uncorked it. Took a sniff. It smelled pretty rough. Strong. Maybe like the alcohol in it had possibly turned. But it also smelled exactly like whatever had been in my cocktail glass for the pre-opening toast. The skin on the back of my neck tightened.

I held the bottle away from my face. Hadn't I seen a man carry a bottle outside in the midst of the festivities at one point? Hadn't I almost said something to Angela? Or was I misremembering something from the evening's commotion?

Maybe it was the night—maybe I was overwhelmed by some sort of feeling of *why not?*—but quite unlike me, I risked it and let curiosity win. I took the tiniest little sip. And in that very moment, I saw it again—the white flash.

This time, the white flash brought with it a warmth— it flowed down my chest, burning my insides like liquor always did. And, oddly enough, that warmth also blew across my face, like a summer breeze.

Scenes from the Bottle

It was summer all around me, my coat instantly too hot, a streak of green beneath my feet. But it was all so blurry—worse, even, than the world usually looked without my glasses. I cringed, squeezing my eyes shut while silver sparks traveled back and forth on the insides of my eyelids.

The warmth that had instantly enveloped me dissolved just as quickly. And a cold breeze attacked yet again, whipping my hair about and tugging it across my face.

I felt myself tumbling, flailing about, the hot and cold oscillating faster and faster. When I next opened my eyes, I found a wintry gray sky above and snow along the edge of the street. But the sun was in the sky instead of the moon. And I wasn't really sure where I was standing anymore. I was still on a town square but it couldn't be Sullivan's. The Page Turner was gone. Ruby's neon sign was gone.

What had just happened?

With a sick twist in my gut, I glanced at the bottle, wondering what had been in it. Was mistletoe poisonous? Had I drunk something that was about to send me to the ER?

14

I staggered down the street a bit, slowly realizing that the people all around me looked as if they'd stepped from some sort of holiday costume party—or maybe the set of a historical play. Women in heels and long skirts, men in suits. And hats. Hats on every head. Beneath the brims, the women had their chin-length hair done in finger waves. Red lipstick adorned their mouths. Behind me, a car horn let out an, "*Ahoooga!*" I stepped to the side, and a Model T sputtered past.

A large woman—bigger than many of the men passing by—stepped through a nearby business's bright green door to prop a sandwich board on the sidewalk. Lunch Special—roast chicken with cornbread dressing, new potatoes and peas, coffee, and a slice of gooseberry pie: 25¢.

"Frankie," a woman greeted, offering a nod of hello.

"Rose," Frankie replied with a similar nod as she finished adjusting her sign.

"I might have heard that Robert Ludlow's garage has hit hard times. Might've heard he was looking for some additional work," Rose said, smoothing one of her gloves, tugging it farther down on her wrist.

"Did you now," Frankie muttered.

"Might. Might *still* be looking for work," Rose said, raising her eyebrows.

"Well. You get him on the line today, you maybe could tell him I have a job for him."

"Here at the diner?"

Frankie stared at Rose awhile. "Well. That'll just have to be between me and Ludlow. You know how this town is. If

15

light bulbs could run on rumors—"

"—Sullivan wouldn't go dark for a thousand years," both women finished in unison.

"And you wouldn't know anything about all that gossip, now would you, Rose? You wouldn't happen to listen in on any of those calls you connect at your switchboard."

"*That*, Frankie, is against the phone company's policy."

"Oh, now, a simple turn of the key, and you'd be able to eavesdrop. Don'tcha ever just get a little curious?"

"Never!" Rose barked, throwing her shoulders back and her nose into the air.

Frankie laughed and waved as she watched Rose hurry on down the sidewalk, toward her job at Southwestern Telephone.

"That's Sullivan for you," I muttered. "Nothing's changed. It's always run on gossip."

Frankie's laughter wound down as she slipped back inside the diner. The door—painted up a familiar bright yellowy green—flopped shut behind her.

I knew that door. I knew that building—the brick walls, that large front window, the placement on the square.

I was staring at Ruby's Place, before it had become Ruby's.

I *was* still in the same town. Just not the same time.

How could that be?

Night fell.

Footsteps clicked behind me. I skittered to the side like a stray cat.

A man passed me, in overalls and an old felt hat. But

something about him snagged my attention. I couldn't just watch him disappear.

I followed him.

At a back door, he leaned forward, whispering a password into a tiny window. The door flew open, and there she stood—the same woman I'd seen earlier with the sandwich board.

"Frankie," the man greeted, tipping his hat. He had a terrible voice. Part misfiring pistons, part injured frog.

"Hey, there, Ludlow," Frankie greeted.

"Got your call," he said. "Extra delivery."

The whispered password, the 1930s-style clothes, the old Model Ts on the streets—no doubt about it, this was Prohibition-era Sullivan. Seemed I'd heard somewhere that before this building was Ruby's Place, it was a diner. At least, it was a diner out front. "Home of the 5¢ steak!" the painted sign advertised on the plate glass window facing the square. Which meant the alley door I was standing next to opened into Frankie's secret speakeasy, the subject of many wild, whispered, romanticized Sullivan tales.

The sound of a woman's singing voice sent the lyrics of "O Christmas Tree" into the alley. Ludlow cocked his head to the side, listening. "Dorothy is in fine form tonight."

A few loud pops sent me cowering. Streams of screaming people thundered out the back door. I ran with them, thoughtlessly, just trying to get away, glass shards crunching beneath my feet.

Daylight broke, and a newspaper blew down the street to tangle about my legs. I grabbed it up to find the front page of the *Sullivan Morning Tribune* covered with the black and white image of police officers with their guns drawn. The diner's plate glass window appeared blown to pieces, scattered on the sidewalk. A headline screamed, "Frankie's Speakeasy Busted on Christmas Eve!"

Time kept ticking by, the days bleeding like seconds, one into the next, the next... Flowers bloomed. Leaves fell. Snow trickled through the air. I tumbled again, feeling the oscillating heat and cold. This time, I knew that seasons were passing as quickly as seconds, one after another, adding up the years.

When it stopped, I swiveled, trying to make sense of what was all around me. When had I wound up this time? My time, or...

I saw her. Ruby herself, her lithe, former-ballerina body pacing the front walk as a work crew installed the red neon Ruby's Place sign.

The newspaper in my hand crinkled against the wind. Glancing down, I realized the front page no longer bore the headline of the bust—and now, the date printed at the top of the page was 1955.

Sure enough, the cars navigating the square had turned sleek, sharp tail fins pointing skyward. Across the street, two men outside Weber's Electronics smoked and glared at the woman who had the nerve to open up shop on their square. Not just any shop—a *bar*.

I frowned at the men, feeling every ounce of Ruby's anger for her.

A large, decorated spruce appeared in the center of the

square. At the same time, a "Grand Opening this Christmas Eve!" sign billowed outside of Ruby's Place. With one sharp snap, the words "Christmas Eve" disappeared. The sign announced instead, "Grand Opening Tonight!"

The front plate glass window—the same that had been shot out during Frankie's speakeasy raid—filled with faces. Celebrating. Toasting. Laughing. Children raced down the sidewalk, passing me by, anxious to get inside.

A woman's voice filled the air, accompanied by a piano. "Dorothy is in fine form tonight," many remarked as the door swung open and shut.

Dorothy had returned. Even though the days of the speakeasy were long gone. She was back, singing for Ruby.

I smiled, taking a few more steps toward the window. A lovely feeling wrapped its arms around me—a cozy Christmas warmth, the kind that often rushed through me anytime I heard Nat King Cole singing of chestnuts and roaring fires. The kind of feeling that came with knowing every person you loved in the world was under the same roof.

The sensation—*the Christmas spirit*—didn't feel fleeting, though. Standing there, staring into Ruby's, with all those faces looking back at me, the emotions of that moment felt more lasting. Sturdier than concrete.

The feeling lasted even as the years slipped by, yet again. The documentary of the town I'd grown up in continued to play out, all around me. Suits gave way to jeans. The Bank of Sullivan was gaining a new addition. Walter Drummond, Vice President of the bank, stood on the sidewalk in his favorite pinstriped wide-collared suit and sideburns, nodding in approval.

A woman's heels clicked on the sidewalk, and Walter turned, offering another nod of approval—at the woman, this time. It wasn't about the way she looked, though she was stunning in her long pleated gray skirt and her white silk blouse, her fitted black leather jacket and her black leather knee boots. Blond updo. Red nails. Walk like a model's.

"Elizabeth," Walter greeted. "Everything going well at the dress shop?"

She grinned, her red lips curling upward in gratitude. "Absolutely. And if it weren't, I'm certain you would see to it that I had everything I needed to make it turn around."

"Ahh, well, everyone deserves a fair shake," Walter said.

"Not everyone feels that way—not when money's on the line," Elizabeth reminded him. "Not when, say, loans are needed to get started."

"Foolish," Walter muttered, shaking his head at the idea, in the same way other businessmen of the time had shaken their heads at his insistence on backing women-run establishments. "You and Ruby are the best investments I ever made."

Signs above the doors of neighboring stores changed, like patterns in an ever-turning kaleidoscope. Openings and closings helped mark the time. The Page Turner appeared behind a banner advertising its own grand opening—readers flocked, anxious to grab the latest bestseller.

I checked the newspaper in my hand again. This time, the front page bore the date 1973.

Beneath the aluminum stars attached to streetlights, a

giant Lincoln pulled up to kiss the curb just outside of Ruby's Place. A young girl hopped out, dressed in red velvet.

"Angela!" a woman shouted, pulling herself from behind the driver's wheel. The same woman, I noticed, who had spoken to Walter earlier. Dressed, this time, in a winter white angora dress coat.

"Hurry, Aunt Elizabeth!" the girl shouted. "We'll miss the whole Christmas Eve!"

"Miss Christmas Eve?" Elizabeth repeated, in a somewhat overexaggerated way. "Why, we can't have that." She raced forward a few steps.

On the sidewalk, Walter nudged a little boy dressed in a three-piece suit nearly identical to his own. The boy hurried to open the door for Elizabeth and Angela.

Boisterous merriment exploded out into the night.

"Thank you, Scott," Elizabeth said. "You and your father are looking absolutely dapper this evening."

When the door fell shut again, the faces—smiling, laughing, singing faces—remained in the front window. Even with their soundtrack muted by the closed door, I could feel my heart dancing to their rhythm.

Still, the scenery moved around me on fast forward, like a time lapse video. But no matter what the season, what the year, faces remained in the front window of Ruby's Place. Smiling, mid-shout, lips curled into song.

At times, their voices grew loud enough to bleed out onto the sidewalk. I saw Evie, the piano player, through the front window—dressed in a sequin jacket. I sang along quietly to the chorus of "White Christmas," and meant it. I really did wish it would snow me in, keep me from leaving. Let me remain an audience of one to the story of Sullivan.

A gust tugged the newspaper from my hand, sent it tumbling down the street. I didn't need to be told the date anymore. These were now the scenes of my own youth, my years wandering the square in my Keds, buying books and CDs. I twirled in place as familiar Christmas decorations began to sparkle yet again. It really was something, getting a chance to walk the streets of my past. I navigated the crowded sidewalk, taking it all in until I bumped someone's shoulder.

"Oooh—sorry," I started, but felt myself stop short when a man smiled at me beneath his dark mustache.

"Just grabbing a couple of last minute gifts for my daughter," he said, before the crowd swallowed him.

"Dad? Dad!" I shouted, but a man carrying a fresh Christmas tree blocked my way, keeping me from catching up.

Dad disappeared, leaving a scrape down the center of my heart.

The entrance to The Page Turner flopped open. I heard skateboard wheels. A teenage boy zipped past me. He had long hair. And a nail in his hand.

"Rob?" I asked.

And then I even saw myself—the teenage me—racing out of the bookstore, trying to catch up to Rob as he sped by on his skateboard. There I was, in my acid washed Palmetto jeans, my heart overflowing as Rob squatted down, bringing the tip of that nail toward the perfectly smooth, wet cement.

I knew what he was about to do. Announce his love for

me to the whole town. Make it permanent—as things always feel permanent when you're sixteen. There his lasting pledge would remain, like a tattoo: *Rob & Geena 4Ever 1987.*

The grownups coming out of stores and getting into nearby cars and attempting to sidestep us on the sidewalk were frowning. Shaking their heads at us. Two foolish kids who didn't know what they were doing.

But they didn't try to erase Rob's words, either.

Suddenly, his hand was in mine, and we were running. Laughing. Because to us, at sixteen, their disapproval and their warnings were ridiculous. *We'll show them.* Doubt is funny, too, when love is real.

With a thud, the square darkened. Like someone had flipped a giant switch. Only the red neon of the Ruby's Place sign remained. But it, too, faded, little by little. Until it disappeared completely. A moon appeared, cutting into the utter blackness. Beneath its hazy glow, a "Closed" sign dangled against the dirty glass of the front window.

Ruby's wasn't closed for the night. It was closed for good. A "For Sale or Lease" sign appeared on the door.

All around me, the crowds thinned on the once-vibrant the square. Passersby no longer bumped into me. I could no longer hear car engines or feet clicking against the sidewalk.

The sun rose and rose again. But storefronts remained dark and empty. Without Ruby's Place, the square took on the look of being a bit run-down and sad.

An older Rob appeared, placing an "Under New Ownership!" sign outside The Page Turner—the bookstore we'd loved as kids, and the same store he had decided to rescue.

Thanks not to one of Walter's loans, but his son Scott's by that time. The Drummond family had passed the torch over at the Bank of Sullivan, one generation to the next.

When skateboard wheels next spun on the pavement, the boy steering his way down the sidewalk was Justin, Rob's teenage son from his long-gone marriage.

The nearby tree lot offered a staggeringly small number of pines for sale. Each tree grew dry and brittle and ignored.

The annual aluminum star decorations disappeared.

I continued to recognize the few faces left to populate the square. Former neighbors who'd come back for a visit. Ex-classmates now grown, with their own spouses and families. And Tina! I nearly called to her. There she was in one of her head-to-toe vintage outfits, pacing the sidewalk in her determination to renovate the then-closed Southwestern Telephone building. She hung her own sign, one that announced she was opening the It Ain't Over Yet flea market. Large console TVs that had once been on display in Weber's Electronics showed up in her front window display, refurbished as fish bowls.

I laughed, watching as she swung her arms about like a traffic cop, helping a couple of delivery guys steer an old switchboard through the front door. "Careful, careful! Can't believe how lucky I was to find it," she was telling them. "That's a switchboard from Sullivan's very own phone company!"

The men steering the moving dolly only grunted. That old switchboard—the same, I somehow felt certain, that Rose had once worked—was nothing but a relic, at that point.

Useless.

Or so it would seem with the quickest of glances.

Through it all—Christmases coming and going and the years flying and the seasons flipping and the changing fashions and the rising and falling of businesses—the faces refused to disappear from the window at Ruby's Place. The images were all still there, holding champagne flutes and cocktail glasses. Looking out at the street. Even though the "For Sale or Lease" sign had been propped outside the door. And even though the place had gone out of business. Who were these people? How did they get in?

I took a few steps forward, gasping when I saw Ruby herself. How could that be? I knew for a fact that the business had been closed by her family after her death. *Just not the same without her*, that was what everyone had said. Nobody was ever going to be quite as good as Ruby at running it.

I had so many questions. Why would the place still be packed? Why would so many still be inside, like it was happy hour, same as always? How was it possible that Ruby's face was still in the window after her business closed? After her death?

A modern sounding car horn blared. An engine roared. A pair of blinding headlights aimed themselves right at me, growing quickly closer.

I yelped and lunged out of the way.

Back to Reality

The car zipped past, taking the ever-changing scenes with it. I stood alone on the sidewalk, holding that old bottle with what I still believed was mistletoe inside it. Feeling certain that, whatever that liquor was, it had allowed me to see a young Rob—the Rob from my past—during our pre-opening toast.

The second sip had taken me back even further. Had let me see the town of Sullivan's memories. Had let me stay long enough to understand the full story of Ruby's Place. And who—or what—those faces in the front window really were.

I suddenly knew everything, even why Angela had come back to town to reopen the old bar. I had a new understanding about Angela and her desire to see her sister again.

I was pretty unsteady on my feet. It had all been so vivid. I might have heard bits and pieces of strange Christmas Eve happenings at Ruby's over the years, but never any indication how it all fit together. And at that moment, the realization could have knocked me over.

Why hasn't all this become legendary? I wondered. In a

small town like Sullivan, there was never any speed limit on a story.

At the other end of the square, the front door to the It Ain't Over Yet flea market flopped open. Tina emerged, wearing a vintage red mouton coat. The hairy ends of the fuzzy material rippled and glowed in the nearby streetlight. Her cat-eye glasses shimmered like moonlight. Her platform shoes clomped against the sidewalk.

Her head swiveled about, one side to another. Was she looking for something? Well—Tina was always looking. Almost like a bird, constantly scavenging. Only, in Tina's world, it was antiques and collectibles she was on the lookout for. Farm auctions, estate sales, dumpster diving. Her Volkswagen was a good fifty years old. Nothing in her wardrobe had come from a new rack in a department store. Her own kitchenware was primarily from the 1940s. And anything she wasn't using herself was for sale at the shop.

She picked something up off the street. Dusted it off. Inspected it in the glow of the streetlight. Even from my distance, I could tell it was a hat. But it didn't seem to satisfy Tina. She continued to look about, kicking at snow piles, hands on her hips.

I hugged the old bottle closer to my chest. After what I'd just seen, it felt like it belonged to me. So I tucked that ancient, dirty bottle inside my coat. I was taking it home.

The door flew open. "Hey, babe," Rob said, throwing his arm around my neck. "You ready to get out of here?" He drew me close, kissing my cheek.

I was. Without a doubt. As we walked, the sky was

every bit as dark as it had been a moment ago. But it didn't really feel like midnight quite as much anymore.

With a sudden surge of excitement and elation, I began to hum "White Christmas" as Rob and I headed toward his truck, certain that bottle had just given me the best Christmas gift I'd ever received:

A story to write.

Words Swirled Like Snowflakes

"You sure you don't want me to come pick you up tomorrow? Or is that today—in a few hours?" Rob asked as the snowflakes danced across the windshield of his truck.

"Positive," I told him as we idled in my driveway. "We already talked about this. You need to spend Christmas Day with Justin." Probably, now that Justin was in his late teens, it was one of the last Christmas Days Rob would get to spend with his son. Maybe, even, the very last. I'd never want to intrude on that, no matter how serious Rob and I were, how permanent we were feeling to each other.

But that wasn't the only reason. It wasn't all selfless. My fingers were also literally itching to get started. All I could think about was being alone—I had far more words bouncing through my head, suddenly, than there were snowflakes swirling through Sullivan. But I also didn't want to hurt Rob's feelings about it.

I kissed him. "Merry Christmas," I said.

"Merry Christmas." He squeezed my fingers as I

popped the passenger side door. The nail I wore on a chain swung forward and thunked against the truck door. A nail with bits of concrete dried to it. The same that Rob had used to carve my name. The same nail on a chain that Rob had given me for Christmas in '89, the last Christmas we'd spent together before Rob headed to the service and I went off to college.

I made my way up the walk, waving at Rob when I stepped into the front hall. I was still feeling a little guilty about sending him off to his own Christmas without me. But I reminded myself Justin was waiting—probably curled up on the couch, under a blanket, the last few scenes of *A Christmas Story* flickering through the living room. Sunrise would wake them both; they'd exchange gifts, make a late breakfast. Justin's girlfriend was out of town with her own family, so there would be no begging on his part to be somewhere else. They'd have the entire day together. To take walks. Stream a few more movies. Just enjoy each other. For Rob, it could be an entire day of freedom from worrying about the store.

And me?

I raced into the living room, tossing my coat in Dad's old easy chair. I booted my laptop, my pulse beating so hard, I could feel it in my earlobes.

It was late—nearly one in the morning. And I'd been working all night, waiting tables. Delivering drinks. Pouring cocoa. But you'd never know it, as revved as I was.

When my computer kicked to life, my fingers attacked the keys.

I knew exactly where I wanted to start.

Because I knew now that I hadn't lost anything. Rob, love, my youth, my dreams, Dad, the town's history—it was all right there, dancing in the air above the square.

Angela was a big part of that—and in the ways of small towns, our tales were all tangled up together.

Yes, in Sullivan, thanks to Angela and Ruby's Place, yesterday wasn't gone. It didn't disappear. It wasn't the past.

It was always.

The Always Story

A Christmas Tale
by Geena Barister

Chapter 1.

A ngela's always story took place at Ruby's.

That's what she called it, anyway: her always story. Because, quite simply, it was the story she *always* relied on. The Christmas tale she'd preserved like an heirloom in a cedar keepsake box. If you think about it, you've got one, too. The story you invariably reach for, taking it out over and over as the years pass. Doesn't matter if the details have maybe gotten a little dated, or if the edges have gone a little yellow. It was still you at your happiest. And it is the story you play over and again in your mind in order to remember what Christmas should be. What's it's been. What you hope it can be again.

Probably, if we were to place the details of our always stories side-by-side, stitch them all together like squares in a quilt, we'd find repeating patterns brimming with red felt chimney stockings and golden, roasted turkeys loaded with sage. Fires would crackle in backgrounds, stoked by sweet smelling logs, flames dancing romantically. We'd stand beneath mistletoe and sit in pews, listening to choirs sing of joy as candlelight cast soft shadows and magic wove itself into the air. Somewhere in the midst of these tales, most if not all of us would find ourselves the recipients of unexpected gifts—both the kind that arrive in shiny wrapped boxes and the kind with no ribbon attached. The sort that involve unexpected gestures of kindness, rushes of love flooding our hearts.

Each telling of such stories is never identical—not even when we're telling the story to ourselves. Our perspective changes. Life pushes us into a different standpoint. We see the past from different angles. But no matter how we frame the events of these tales, we rely on always stories to bring back the time when the holiday spirit invaded us, took over, hijacked our very soul, and made the whole world seem a place brimming with goodwill. When our younger selves were within reach and the future sparkled like twinkle lights.

Angela's own always story, the one about to unfold, involves far more than a single holiday season. It is a story she has never shared fully. Only fragments of it. Little sketches—like the time when she was eight, and wore her favorite red velvet dress—or fourteen, the last Christmas she spent with her Aunt Elizabeth. She's chimed in a few sentences here and there, mostly when a gathering of acquaintances was in the midst of rehashing their own Christmas remembrances.

But the truth is, Angela's always story spans nearly the entirety of her life so far. And requires far more than a few sentences. It unfolds not by the usual warm hearth, but in a bar.

The quickest of glances would indicate there is nothing about Ruby's Place to remind anyone of Christmas at all. It's yet another old brick building on the square of a small old Midwestern town illuminated by yet another old neon sign.

But if we should pause for a while, on the sidewalk

outside—and if we were to rely on our hearts' eyes—we would notice the bright green front door, clearly refreshed with a new coat of paint and adorned with a fragrant pine wreath. We would pick up the lingering sweet scent of Ruby's signature homemade marshmallows, the perfect addition to her cocoa recipe. Slowly, we would begin to feel a tingle, a reawakening—a rash of goosebumps on the back of the neck.

Even without yet knowing the full history of the building or the details of Angela's story, it is easy to tell something *is* different about Ruby's Place. And not just because a bar with cocoa and marshmallows on the menu is highly unusual. The longer we stand, the easier we will find it to believe her decades-long always story took place here. And though a "Closed" sign is turned toward the street, curiosity will inevitably draw us close enough to cup our hands around our eyes as we attempt a better glimpse at what's inside.

I know it's dark, but just stand still a moment. Squint if you need to. You can see it begin to play out, can't you? No? Let me help. It all began with Angela's first visit to Ruby's Place. Christmas Eve, 1972…

Chapter 2.

"**H**ow is she?" Ruby asked, leaning her elbows on the bar. Elizabeth sighed, shaking her head as she glimpsed back at her niece, her little Angela, standing in the center of the bar. Refusing to take a seat. Or join in any of the festivities. "Maybe this was a bad idea," she muttered as she patted the back of her blond updo.

Elizabeth had a well-deserved reputation for being the biggest clotheshorse in Sullivan, never leaving her house without perfectly tailored dresses and silk stockings and the flashiest jewelry suites—elaborate handwired Miriam Haskell necklaces and clip earrings. Long red nails. Always smelling of Cashmere Bouquet powder.

"She even sleeps in designer hair rollers," Elizabeth had overheard—more than once—as she'd stopped to purchase her morning paper from the newsstand.

"…movie star satin robes," was another such rumor. "Flutter out behind the gal as she streaks between the rooms of her house. Can see her sometimes through the window. When the drapes aren't pulled."

"Well. She needs to look good even at night. Hear she's got a movie star *boyfriend*. A real celebrity. The kind that's used to women lookin' good even in their sleep."

That one—uttered earlier that very morning—had made Elizabeth bark a surprised laugh. She'd just kept on snorting, all the way from the newsstand to her dress store. Had to get there early for the last shopping day before Christmas.

She snorted again, sitting at the bar, remembering. But it was all in good fun. She knew that no matter how wrong the people of Sullivan usually were about her own private life, no one really saw her flamboyance as a weakness, as vanity. Mostly because she did own the most popular women's clothing store in town. The ladies all flocked to her store to purchase something special for their holiday nights out. And on Christmas Eve, for Ruby's Place, Elizabeth herself pulled out all the stops. The year before, she'd arrived to the bar with a peacock feather in her crushed velvet hat. Elizabeth had an artistic eye, they all said. A way of putting things together. It was not frivolous; it was simply who she was.

Of course, by then—1972—fashion had grown decidedly more relaxed, more and more informal. But thanks to Elizabeth, though collars were wider and the skirts often shorter, on Christmas Eve, shoes were still polished and ready for dancing. Shiny polyester fabrics showed off bright splashes of color on scarves and ties. And there was also still something about Ruby's Place that made everyone reach for a classic finishing touch, one that had been in their drawers or jewelry boxes for ages: grandmother's pearls, maybe, or inherited gold cufflinks. A pocket square. They smelled of their very best perfume. The town of Sullivan had never been overly prosperous, but everyone had some sort of special trinket, tucked away in a drawer or the back of the closet, wrapped in tissue paper. On Christmas Eve at Ruby's, those special bobbles had never looked better. They all vied for a nod of approval from Elizabeth, because it meant the town's haute couture expert agreed.

Ruby craned her neck to get a better look over Elizabeth's shoulder. It wasn't easy—that shoulder had been adorned with a large black organza-covered puff sleeve and an oversized poinsettia pin made of red silk petals and green glass leaves.

But there she was, Elizabeth's niece, standing in the midst of the bar's Christmas Eve bustle, looking as if she could cry at any moment. The sour expression on little seven-year-old Angela's face was deeply uncharacteristic, especially for a girl her age at this time of the year. The frown was also a shame, Ruby caught herself thinking, considering that Angela was absolutely decked out, as Ruby'd expected her to be. In her silver dress and shoes—a gift from Elizabeth's chic dress shop—Angela looked either like a disco ball or maybe one of those aluminum stars the Sullivan City Council had attached to the streetlights on the square early in December.

"What's with the hat?" Ruby asked, giggling softly, still staring at Angela. She'd chosen to top her pretty new outfit with an awful brown stocking cap. Handmade. Had to be. Alternating rows of knit and purl stitches were clumsy and uneven—some, you could tell, had been dropped and awkwardly reincorporated. Clearly, it had been someone's first attempt at making a hat. And to make matters worse, it was far too big, circling down below her eyebrows and hanging loosely around her ears.

Elizabeth gave Ruby a look.

Ruby, Elizabeth's best friend, only grunted in understanding. The two women had been reading each other's looks ever since Ruby'd shown up in the midst of the Eisenhower administration to purchase the empty space, renovate it into something splendid and special. Theirs was the kind of friendship hard to find at what anyone else would have called late in life (our "second halves," as Elizabeth often phrased it). Both single, both business owners, both trying to forge their own ways, carve out careers and lives on their own terms, even though the odds were against them. It never happened that way, not past youth. Schoolchildren had the luxury of being surrounded by entire classrooms of kids all at the same stage of life, all dealing with the same rules, the same milestones: lost teeth, first kisses, learning to drive. It was comfortable and reassuring, experiencing life in those familiar clumps. But once they reached adulthood and separated from the schoolyard, they found themselves interacting with people of all different ages and in different stages of life. Facing struggles and milestones at odds with their own. Friendships, as a result, tended to be fragile and short-lived; they existed only on the surface, like a coat of lipstick.

Not so with Ruby and Elizabeth.

Ruby squeezed her friend's arm. She knew the complete story about Angela's ugly knit hat, just by looking at Elizabeth. The sloppy, unsightly thing had been made by Angela's sister.

And Angela's sister was exactly what Elizabeth had brought Angela here to forget. At least for a little while.

"Pour you a champagne, kid?" Ruby asked, relying on the nickname she'd always used for Elizabeth. *Kid*, a word that had always made Elizabeth chuckle.

Not this night, though.

"Pfff," Elizabeth muttered, tossing a hand covered in long red fingernails. "This night doesn't exactly feel celebratory."

"Make it for you anyway. It's your favorite," Ruby said and retrieved one of the bottles she kept just for Elizabeth. A former ballerina, Ruby was nothing like the stereotypical picture of a barmaid—no rough looking woman with a smoker's voice, face wrinkled by hardships. She was lovely, lithe, still moving effortlessly years after her last curtain call and long after her chestnut bun had turned white. Her slender body reminded most of her customers of their favorite screen star, Audrey Hepburn, a name some even teased her with.

Elizabeth glared at the flute of champagne that appeared under her nose. She had imagined this night would transform her little niece's attitude, the same way that the right dress could transform a woman. She'd seen it over and over in her shop: the right cut of a skirt, the right shoe could invigorate even the most downtrodden individual. Turn her into someone confident and shiny and new.

Fingers crossed, just minutes ago, upon arriving, Elizabeth had hung Angela's little coat on the hook beside the door, patted her on the shoulder, and sent her out to join the group of kids gathered around the piano. "A sing-along!" she'd said with a smile. "What fun is that!"

But Angela had simply planted her feet in the center of the room—a good six feet or so away from the piano—refusing to take a step closer.

"Poor thing," Theresa Vargas muttered, watching from across the room.

"I heard," her sister Vera agreed. "Such a tragedy."

Elizabeth grimaced listening in on the women's conversation, guilt settling like stones in her stomach. It appeared this night was never going to allow Angela to escape (even momentarily) what had made her mouth turn downward in the first place: Angela's sister, Gail, had died the summer before.

Such a blunt statement. *Gail died.* Like a whack from a ball-peen hammer. But there was really no other way to phrase it. No way to soften the reality. At seventeen, beautiful and smart, everything had seemed easy for Gail. That really never was completely true for anyone, Elizabeth knew. It was just a way to dismiss someone who was excelling: *Oh, well, it's easy for them.* Like somehow life came more naturally to others, some had a talent at just being themselves.

Everyone struggled. Everyone took their knocks, got their hearts broken, felt disappointment. But Gail had been the sort to recover quickly. She ran track and field— cross-country. That was Gail—the sort to go the distance, no matter the terrain.

Until the boating accident last July. Until Gail was overpowered by an angry lake. A freak summer storm popping up out of nowhere. An outing with friends for the holiday that had ended in tragedy.

"Looks a little like she's treading water, doesn't she?" Theresa continued, seemingly unaware of how cold-blooded that sounded. Or how close Elizabeth was sitting—well within earshot.

Elizabeth flinched. Should she have asked Angela to leave the hat in the car? Angela had been clutching it, stuffing it in pockets, carrying it in her backpack since the truly awful process of reorganizing and cleaning had arrived at her home, just as it always arrived following any death. This time, everyone in Angela's family was trying to figure out what to do with Gail's sneakers and her hair combs and her records.

What was important? What could they let go of? What would they miss? What if they made a mistake and threw away something they'd want later on?

To little Angela, everything was important: a broken music box, a paper from her sophomore year English class, her first attempt at a knitting project for home economics.

And now, here she was, *wearing* that awful brown hat.

Elizabeth felt horrible. This was the wrong thing to do. It was too soon.

And yet—it was Christmas. It was bound to be a hard Christmas for Angela. Far harder than any seven-year-old should have to endure. But there should still be gladness, too. Elizabeth had wanted to show Angela that. She dug her red nails into her palms. Perhaps there was a great deal of truth in Theresa's words. Perhaps she had expected too much from her niece. Perhaps she had wrongly anticipated that she, too, would be able to recover just as quickly as her sister. Go the distance, keep pushing forward, even when her entire body hurt. Even when she felt like she was on fire and ready to collapse.

Yes, she thought sadly, that was far too much to expect from a seven-year-old.

Maybe, she thought, they'd just have a treat and leave. Pat Theresa on the shoulder on the way out, wordlessly thanking her for her indirect advice.

Winking, she curled her finger, motioning for the child to join her at the bar.

Angela dragged herself across the floor. Elizabeth stood, stuck her hands under Angela's arms, and hoisted her onto the barstool beside her.

"Pick your poison," Ruby encouraged Angela.

Angela looked tiny on the stool. Almost as if she were shrinking. She sat motionless, offering no response.

Elizabeth wordlessly begged Ruby for help.

Ruby responded by quickly whipping up a cup of hot chocolate. "This is my own personal recipe," she boasted. "See these marshmallows?" She pointed at the white toasted lumps on top. "Made them myself."

Angela just stared.

"Don't let it get cold, now," Ruby protested. "That's not that powdered stuff from a packet. That's the real deal."

But Angela only sighed, refusing to take so much as the tiniest of sips. That word—*real*—echoed painfully in her head. Her sister had been real, but by then, she wasn't any-more. *Real.* What was so great about it? Just because something was real didn't make it safe. She crossed her arms over her chest, as though to protect her young heart.

Chapter 3.

On the opposite side of the room, the piano player, Evie, pounded out a series of loud, finale-style chords and rose from the bench, her sequined jacket catching the lights. "Fifteen minute break!" she announced. "Everybody decide what you want to sing during the next set."

The children scattered; when they reached the tables where their parents lingered, drinking coffee and cocktails or savoring the last few bites of a prime rib dinner, they were given paper money for the tip jar poised on the top of the ornate upright piano.

Evie would empty that jar five times that night. And she'd divide it fifty-fifty with Dorothy, the bar's lone singer.

Not that Dorothy cared about the money. Not on Christmas Eve. She'd find a way to slip her share in Evie's jacket before the night was through.

As Evie headed toward the restroom, Dorothy remained beside the piano, a picture of fashion herself in a burgundy velvet pantsuit, a gardenia tucked behind one ear. She enjoyed watching the kids scamper back and forth.

Without music, Ruby's Place filled with laughter and shouts, tinkling glasses. The front door swung open again and again. Boughs of mistletoe dangled from fingertips. Kisses were planted on the cheeks of friends. Presents were exchanged. Cameras emerged and passersby were asked to take pictures of entire families—three, four generations—all gathered at the same table.

Someone, Dorothy knew as her eyes bounced through the crowded room, would open a ring box and get down on one knee. She could usually guess who it would be—nerves were a dead giveaway on a man—but tonight, she wasn't sure. She only knew that she and Evie would cheer with the rest of the crowd before offering their own rendition of the current most popular love song (this year, probably "The First Time Ever I Saw Your Face"), while the newly engaged couple took a twirl of their own on the dance floor. The whole bar stopped for the just-engaged couples—Ruby turned down the lights and the onlookers grew misty-eyed.

"Let's see…" Dorothy muttered, scanning the room, playing this yearly guessing game with herself. But she stopped, zeroing in on a little girl at the bar. Staring at a cup of cocoa as Elizabeth and Ruby leaned ever closer, trying to coax her into tasting it.

Dorothy cocked her head, her heart hurting for the girl. The thing was, everybody glittered on Christmas Eve. That night, same as any other Christmas, they'd arrived absolutely wrapped—not just in tinsel or fancy fabric, but in jubilance. Everybody except that little girl, anyway.

Maybe Elizabeth and Ruby were good at reading each

other's faces. Maybe their friendship had given them that understanding. But maybe they weren't so good at reading the little girl. Luckily for them, Dorothy was especially good at reading one particular kind of expression. She could recognize it instantly, on anyone. Even if she had just met that person. It was, in short, the look of grief. Of missing one special someone. And it was definitely the look Angela wore.

She pulled herself away from the piano and weaved through the crowd. At the bar, she smiled at Ruby, who appeared uncharacteristically frustrated. "Hey, Rubes," Dorothy said. "Did you happen to hear some bells in the middle of my last song?"

"Bells?"

Dorothy winked.

"Bells!" Ruby said, playing along. "You know, the chorus was kind of loud, but yes, I think I did. Faintly."

"It is about the right time for Santa to show up, isn't it?" Elizabeth agreed, checking her watch.

"Why don't we go outside and take a look?" Dorothy asked Angela, holding out her hand.

Angela stared at her fingers a moment. Dorothy was a complete stranger, and under ordinary circumstances, a girl Angela's age would refuse and lean in closer to her Aunt Elizabeth, in a kind of silent request for protection.

That night, Angela gently placed her hand in Dorothy's and allowed her to help her off the stool.

Elizabeth might have found that inexplicable, but Dorothy'd expected it. When you were feeling the way Angela obviously was, you would take any opportunity to leave—

leave the room, leave a building, leave the neighborhood. It always felt like an opportunity to leave behind your heavy heart.

You didn't, though. You never did. A heavy heart went everywhere with you. Dorothy knew that, too.

Maybe, though, Dorothy thought, she could offer the girl a little bit of solace.

She led Angela down a small bricked hallway, toward an alley door.

Outside, the air smelled of impending snow. Dorothy tilted her head, as though attempting to listen.

"You don't hear him," Angela muttered. "Not Santa."

"How do you know?"

"I know." She slumped onto the bottom step. The way she said it, Dorothy assumed Angela was also saying that there was no such thing as Santa Claus. Or magic. Or wonder.

Which meant, by extension, there was no real hope.

It would be a terrible thing for a girl so young to lose her belief in possibility. To think that good things could never happen to her.

Dorothy sat on the step and tapped Angela's shoulder. "Look here," she insisted, pointing at a series of small holes along the old wooden door.

Angela swiveled. "What are those things?" She pushed her hat up higher on her forehead to get a better look.

Dorothy leaned in close. "Bullet holes," she whispered.

Angela jerked backward. "No way."

"They are," Dorothy insisted. "Before Ruby owned this place, it was a speakeasy."

"A what?"

"A speakeasy. Back a long, long time ago, drinking liquor used to be illegal. So they had to hide the bars. Had to whisper a password through the window in this door up there—" she paused to point "—in order to get in. A woman named Frankie Hall ran it. One Christmas Eve, there was a huge shootout. The speakeasy was shut down. Frankie went on the run with one of her bartenders."

Dorothy asked herself why she'd just told her so much. Was it too much for a first grader to take in?

"How do you know that?"

Dorothy grinned. It wasn't too much. "I was the singer. I worked for Frankie."

Angela's eyes swelled with surprise. "You did not."

"I did too. You see that picture of the singer inside? Behind the bar?"

"That's a pretty lady in a fancy hat."

"That's *me*. And that hat is called a cloche. Used to be all the rage. Sometimes, when the mood hits right, I pull my old hat out and wear it again."

To prove her point, Dorothy put her hands on her hips and stuck her chin out, mimicking the pose she'd struck in that long-ago picture. "Need the hat, though, don't I?" she asked. "Hats can make all the difference."

Angela squirmed, pushing her own knit hat back on her forehead.

"My husband played music here, too," Dorothy added, nudging Angela with her elbow. "He played trumpet."

"What's his name?"

"Chester. It was, anyway."

"Was?" Angela's hat slipped, ready to swallow her right eye.

"He left during the Depression. A time—" Her eye darted out toward Angela. This, she felt certain, really was too much. No need for a long-winded economics lesson. "Well. He went off to find a job in another town. A better way to make a living than working in a speakeasy. An honest job. One that would let us really have all the things we wanted in life." Dorothy grew a bit heavy as her voice trembled.

"Like what?" Angela pressed.

"Oh, a family. Little house, maybe. All grown-ups have different versions of the same dream."

Angela kept staring. Intently.

"He didn't come back," Dorothy said.

"Ever?"

"It happened a lot back then. Times were hard all over the country. I waited such a long time for him to come home."

Angela nodded. "I keep waiting for my sister to come back, too," she whispered. "But she can't."

"What happened?"

"She was just supposed to be gone for the weekend," she squeaked, hugging her knees. "But the boat turned over. And they said it was too dark to find her. Nobody told me that to my face, though. I had to hear it hiding on the stairs."

"Maybe they just didn't want to hurt you."

"Wouldn't you have been glad if somebody'd told you what really happened to Chester?"

Dorothy was struck by what an adult thought that really was. Here she was, a little girl who seemed to still want to believe in Santa—whose eyes kept darting up to the starry sky, trying to make out his sled—but who had endured a horrible tragedy. The kind that made a person grow up too fast. Or parts of a person, anyway.

"It feels wrong," Angela said. "Being here. Having a good time. When my sister can't."

Dorothy nodded. She tugged her velvet jacket tighter. It was awfully cold outside sitting on a concrete step.

"I have a secret," Dorothy whispered, her breath making clouds in the night air. In truth, it was not so much a secret as a daydream. A wish. A *wouldn't it be lovely if...* But it had carried her through all these years without Chester. And she felt certain it would carry Angela now.

Angela stuck a finger through her knit hat to scratch her forehead. Her sister had used the itchiest wool on the planet.

Dorothy nudged her. "Don't you want to hear it?"

Angela shrugged.

"Ruby's Place is magical."

"There's no such thing as magic," Angela grumbled.

Dorothy clutched her chest as if she'd been shot with the child's words, the same way the poor door had once been shot full of bullets. She began her story, speaking softly, meaningfully:

"You're wrong. There's magic inside these walls. I know. Ruby hired me to sing here when she bought the place. Really took a chance on me. Hired me before I'd ever sung a note in front of her! But it made me so sad. All I could think about was the way Chester and I had once played here, during the speakeasy days. And how it seemed like Ruby wasn't just sprucing the place up. Felt more to me like she was erasing Chester."

"My parents cleaned out my sister's room," Angela muttered. "And then we moved. Somebody else lives there now. I didn't want to leave. It didn't feel right."

"*Listen*," Dorothy said, feeling like she had really snagged Angela, "I told you Ruby hired me on the spot. Without even hearing me sing. Why do you think she'd do that?"

"Maybe she felt sorry for you, being so old and all."

Dorothy swallowed a giggle. "Maybe," she corrected, "she knew I needed help."

"What's the difference?" Angela moped.

"Oh, there's a *big* difference." Dorothy's teacher voice suddenly kicked in. She had spent decades teaching would-be singers and pianists. Private lessons. High school choir. Elementary school introductory band. Making a musician, she had learned, required far more than learning the difference between eighth notes and half rests.

Mostly, it was about encouragement. Enthusiasm. To learn to play music, a student had to believe. As a result, Dorothy had become something of a belief expert.

So she knew, sitting on that cold step, she could convince Angela to believe as well.

"When you feel sorry for someone," Dorothy said, drawing her mouth down, "well, that's because there's no hope they can change. No more opportunities. End of the road. But if somebody only needs a little help," she went on, straightening up and throwing her shoulders back, "well, then, there *is* hope. They just need a little direction. They need to be shown the way."

"It doesn't matter, anyway. This is totally different. I can't sing."

Dorothy belly laughed. "You didn't let me tell you the important part. It wasn't about the job, don't you see? It was about Chester. It was about the magic of this very building. On Christmas Eve."

Angela plopped her elbows on her knees.

"Oh, I know," Dorothy went on. "I know. I've sat right in your spot. I know that you feel like there will never be a happy Christmas again. But I'm here to tell you that this building just kept on. Christmas after Christmas. Even after being shot full of bullet holes." She stuck her finger in a hole in the door to illustrate. "When you survive something hard, something scary, it changes you. Not always in bad ways. This building survived a horrible night, many years ago. And now, it's able to grant wishes on Christmas Eve."

Angela's eyes grew far away. Was she even still listening?

"It granted my wish. Want to know what it was?"

Angela nodded.

Dorothy worked her jaw, darting her eyes about. "This should be between you and me. This secret is so sweet—if it gets out, it could destroy everything. This town is so full of gossipers."

"I know!" Angela hissed back. Her eyes were growing bright for the first time. "If light bulbs could run on rumors,

Sullivan wouldn't go dark for a thousand years. My dad says that all the time."

"It's true, it's true. But I can trust you, can't I? With the truth?"

"Yes. I keep secrets."

Dorothy nodded. "I can tell. I can see it on you. You really are good at keeping them."

Angela nodded eagerly.

"At the end of my first night, Ruby asked me to stay awhile. After everyone else had gone home. I was a little afraid she was going to fire me. But she smiled at me in a way that said *she* had a secret. One she was going to share with me.

"She asked me what Chester liked to drink. I didn't quite know what to say. Why, Chester wasn't much of a drinker. But you know, Ruby, she makes this cocoa here that is just delicious. And I knew Chester would have loved that."

"She made me a cup!" Angela exclaimed.

"She did?"

"Yes!"

"Well," Dorothy said. "Ruby, she poured two cups. She carried them to a table in the back. She brought me an extra plate of marshmallows. Dimmed the lights. Made sure the candle on my table was lit. And then she left."

Dorothy paused to smile. "But I wasn't alone."

Angela's chest heaved with breath. "What? What happened?"

"Chester," Dorothy whispered, taking Angela's hand. "There he was. My Chester. On the opposite side of the table. Together, we drank our cocoa and we talked. Oh, it was so good to see him. We talked about everything. We spent the rest of the night right there. It was the best present I ever received. And you want to know something else?"

"What?"

"I get that same present every year."

"Will you tonight?"

Dorothy nodded.

Angela jumped to her feet, already lunging for the door.

"Wait!" Dorothy said, grabbing onto Angela's wrist. "It's our secret, right? You mustn't tell anyone. We don't need it to get out. Get everywhere." She held her breath, waiting for Angela's response. She didn't want Angela talking it up, letting others convince her that this story of Dorothy's was a bunch of made-up fantasy. That it could never happen.

A girl, she felt, was entitled to a little belief in the impossible. Wasn't that what Christmas was all about?

Angela nodded and bolted inside.

Dorothy hurried in as well, keeping the kind of distance that allowed her watch what was about to unfold.

Chapter 4.

Angela raced to the bar. "Ruby!" she shouted, waving to get the bartender's attention. She pushed her hat back from her forehead, attempting to free up her eyes, but the hat only tumbled back down.

"I need another cup! And a whole plate of marshmallows," she said.

"What's gotten into you—" Elizabeth started. But when she caught Dorothy's eye, Dorothy placed a finger to her lips.

So Elizabeth just leaned back and picked up her champagne flute, already marked with red lipstick. Acted as though Angela could take care of whatever this was herself.

All while watching her niece's every move.

Ruby placed a second cup and a saucer of toasted homemade marshmallows on the bar.

Angela pushed her hat back again, her face flushed as she glanced about the back of the bar. Somehow, a tiny table for two remained empty. Perhaps because it was in a darkened corner. Perhaps because everyone seemed to have arrived in large groups, parties.

Then again, maybe it was waiting just for her.

The why didn't matter, though. Not then.

"I need a tray!" she called over the din. Then, because it sounded a little rude and demanding, added a polite, "Please?"

Ruby loaded a tray with the marshmallows and two cups of cocoa and circled around to help Angela balance it with both hands.

"Maybe you should let Ruby carry that—" Elizabeth started, but Ruby shot her a look that said it would be fine, whatever happened. Spilled cocoa could clean up every bit as easily as somebody's spilled gin and tonic.

The three women watched as Angela dipped and ducked and steered her way through the crowd. At the back corner table, she placed a cup in front of each chair. Put the marshmallows in the middle. Slid the tray under the table.

Angela's heart beat so hard she was almost dizzy as she slid into her chair. She squeezed her eyes shut. "Please, please, please," she muttered.

When she opened them again, a young woman was sitting in the chair on the opposite side of the table. She was staring away from Angela, through the nearby plate glass, toward the street outside.

"Don't sit there," the girl warned, without looking at Angela. "I've been saving that seat for someone all night. She should be here soon."

"Who are you waiting for?" Angela asked.

Still without looking Angela's way, the young woman pointed toward the redbird on the windowsill. "Cardinals appear—"

"—when angels are near," Angela finished. "Your favorite saying. It's why you insisted Mom and Dad name me Angela. Your little—"

Finally, the girl turned to look. "There you are!" Gail exclaimed. "My little angel. Never thought you'd get here."

Angela smiled. She pushed a cup of cocoa closer to Gail. "Got you one of your own. And extra marshmallows."

Gail smiled, taking her first sip. "It's pretty hot," she said. "Blow first. Don't let it burn your mouth."

But Angela only giggled, even as a tear escaped one of her eyes. Maybe it had only been a wish for Dorothy, but it was real for Angela, who was still so young that her belief in the seemingly impossible—while shaken—was still more easily accessible. She knew, as she sat there with her sister, that nothing would ever burn her again.

On the other side of the room, Dorothy's eyes filled with happy tears. It really had happened! There the two sisters were, gleefully chatting away. Dorothy's own belief swelled inside of her. One of these days, she knew, she would see her Chester again too.

That belief would carry her through the next year. And the one after that.

Such was the power of belief.

Chapter 5.

Forty-plus years later (2017, if you want to be precise), faced with another fast-approaching holiday season, Angela locked her front door and raced out into the night. But she wasn't quite sure where she was going when she climbed in her car. Her headlights made nothing clearer.

It was a terrible car, rusted out, with a busted taillight and nearly bald tires and the kind of miles on it that meant there were surely parts wearing out under the hood. Lots of parts. At this point, Angela was afraid to change the air filter or even add new windshield wiper fluid. She didn't want to look. Or be stuck sinking a pile of her available cash into another hunk of metal. She had been saving for ages, always for some big future event, though she'd never been sure what.

At fifty-two years old, Angela felt she also had a few too many miles on her. More than a few worn-out parts of her own. And the worst of all her broken parts—the one doing the most crying out for immediate attention, the part whose malfunction threatened to send everything else inside of her spinning into a rather disastrous state—was the interior crank that had once charged her beliefs. What was that, exactly? A human alternator for the heart, maybe.

She was not quite sure when that part had officially conked out. Had her belief still been glowing last year? Dimly, but still flickering? Somehow, it was hard to remember. The same way it was hard to remember whether it had snowed the year before or not.

At an intersection, Angela paused to study herself in her rearview mirror. Grayer and heavier than she would have liked, sure. But the worst part was, it wasn't just her reflection but her entire life that felt like it had been shunted into the rearview mirror—her youth, every opportunity for success. What had she accomplished? What had she done? No great career, an apartment filled with furniture she had purchased nearly thirty years ago, a bitter and broken engagement. How cruel the world had been to her, tricking her into trusting there'd be a multitude of chances as the years went by. Only to get here, with nothing to claim success for. Nothing to fulfill her.

What a disappointment she had become to herself. At the time of year when attention turned to shiny new things, Angela felt as though she would never have another shiny new thing again.

Shiny new things were for young people. The lives of women her age were fixed items, set in concrete. Like sidewalks. The kind of sidewalks young people walked right across, dragging heavy two-wheelers loaded with their own chances, never once bothering to look down and see the Angelas of the world beneath their feet. At least, not until the weight of everybody else's travels and chances at happiness made cracks begin to form in all the Angelas. *Then*, women her age were cursed for being bumpy and rugged and making those young people stub their toes.

If something truly wonderful or exciting or life-altering were to happen to her, it already would have. The time for change was up there in the rearview too.

It was a sour way to feel this time of year. She told herself she was being ridiculously sullen, like a child moping because she hadn't gotten the present she wanted. But she could not shake the feeling. It had infected her. Her tightened-up throat hurt. She could find no happiness in the season.

She tilted the mirror, and there it was: the old knit hat. The one her sister had made. She hadn't worn it in years, but today, for some reason, she'd dug it out and put it on. The wool scratched against her forehead. It smelled a bit musty, like the dresser drawers she never much opened because they were filled with the pantyhose she no longer seemed to need.

She missed her sister Gail. Thoughts of her had appeared recently, seemingly out of nowhere, also smelling musty, like they had been in storage. Gail would be retired by now. Often, lately, Angela caught herself trying to picture what Gail would have become—and maybe even what Angela might have become had everything been different, including Gail not going to the lake that July day. It was a lie to say that a long life was a finished life; Angela knew that. We all come into the world in the middle of our parents' stories, and we leave in the middle of our own. No matter what our age.

But somehow, that Christmas, seventeen seemed especially cruel.

The car groaned as Angela drove aimlessly, not even quite sure what she was looking for.

When the gas gauge grew dangerously low, she pulled into an old Texaco station. After filling the tank, she went into the attached convenience store and milled around the aisles, looking for something additional to buy. Something that would offer an excuse, some reason why she had come inside rather than paying at the pump. Something that disguised just how much Angela was in need of some human interaction.

The interior of the station had been decorated with green tinsel and red plastic bells. The nightcrawler cooler, now adorned with weird felt reindeer antlers, was empty and had been scrubbed clean months ago. The fluorescent lights were buzzing like outdoor bug zappers. Alvin and the rest of the Chipmunks were singing through static about Christmastime being here and wanting a hula hoop. This place seemed as anxious to get past Christmas—and back to the summer months—as she was.

Except, where would Angela be in the summer? Not miraculously someplace different. That much was clear.

Angela groaned and reached for some antacid. This was a mistake. She shouldn't have come.

"What's your position on fruitcake?"

Angela turned to find the woman at the checkout counter staring her way. Clearly that fruitcake question had been aimed at her. The clerk had her hands on her hips and she was gnawing a wad of gum in an overexaggerated way, the

old cow-with-cud move. She wore a Christmas-themed turtleneck under her White Squirrel Gas Station smock.

Angela shook her head, feeling fuzzy and sad and unsure how to respond.

The woman pointed at a table filled with what appeared to be tiny homemade loaves, each one Saran-wrapped.
"Only a buck apiece."

"I'll take one," Angela said.

"Just one?" the woman pleaded.

"My sister was the one who liked fruitcake," Angela
said softly. Her hat seemed to respond by getting increasingly,
furiously itchier as she dragged herself toward the table.

"Three it is," the woman announced triumphantly.

Angela started to protest, but the woman shook her
head. "On the house," she insisted. "Made 'em myself, but I
overestimated the number of folks out there who actually like
the stuff."

Angela hadn't meant to hurt the woman's feelings.
"Crack one of those open," she said, making her way to the
cappuccino dispenser. "I haven't tried it in ages. Not since—"
her voice trailed. Not since she was a kid. And her sister'd
conned her into it. She filled a Styrofoam cup.

"Getting awful late," the woman observed. Her
nametag read, "Cyndi."

Angela nodded, agreeing to more than just the time of
day. She was late for everything: love, achievement, happiness.
If Gail were still around, she would still be a sister. But it was
too late for that, too. She was so tired of feeling this way.

"You off to visit somebody? How much more drive

you got yet?"

"Not sure. Where am I, exactly?"

"'Bout ten miles from Sullivan."

"Really?" Angela was so surprised she overfilled her cappuccino cup. She yelped as the hot liquid hit her fingertips. She put her cup down and shook coffee droplets from her hand, admitting, "I grew up there. Must have lost track of where I was."

"You're kiddin'." Cyndi plopped two cellophane-wrapped plastic forks on the counter and spread out some paper napkins. She squinted at Angela.

"You don't recognize me," Angela supposed.

"Not right off."

"You've lived in Sullivan your whole life."

"Pretty much."

"My name is Angela Lowe—which I'm guessing by the look on your face doesn't ring an immediate bell, either."

"Nope."

"And now, you're going back through all the Sullivan stories you've heard, trying to remember anything at all about a woman my age, somebody young in the seventies and eighties. I mean, surely, you must know something. If light bulbs could run on rumors—"

"—Sullivan wouldn't go dark for a thousand years," the two women finished in unison.

They dissolved for a moment into laughter.

"Believe it or not," Cyndi said, "You're walking distance from Old Scroggin's Mountain."

"—which was never really a mountain, but a great

sledding hill," Angela said, to prove she knew the place.

"Lots of fun times out there," Cyndi agreed. "A few bloody and banged up limbs here and there, too," she laughed. "To be a kid, eh?"

"—or not so much a kid anymore," Angela agreed. Everyone had gone out there after a snow. Even grownups took their turns.

"You got a good memory," Cyndi remarked.

"Sullivan was important to me," Angela admitted. "My Aunt Elizabeth owned the dress shop there for ages."

"Oh, yeah!" Cyndi pointed at her with her fork. "Elizabeth. That lady was so swanky. I heard tell she wore hair rollers with diamonds in 'em."

"I heard that one, too."

"Is it true?"

"I'd never want to spoil the illusion," Angela said.

"What was that other story about her?" Cyndi wrinkled her forehead. "Had a secret beau. That was it! Never did hear who. Assumed it was somebody from New York or Paris or something. Maybe a celebrity."

Angela laughed. "She always reminded me of a movie star," she admitted. "When I was little, I'd dreamed of growing up to be just like her."

Cyndi's smile faded as her eyes bounced across Angela. Things got awkward as she seemed to make note that Angela was nothing like a movie star. That fact sort of hung there, like a smelly rug that had been strung outside to be aired out.

"So. What brings you this time?" Cyndi asked. "Can't be…" Her voice trailed. Elizabeth and her dress store were long gone. That unspoken fact hung in the air, too, right alongside Angela's un-movie-star-ness, the smell of the just-unwrapped fruitcake, the high-pitched sounds of Alvin and the Chipmunks, and the hum of the lights.

Cyndi frowned. "You okay?"

Angela nodded, but it was all so overpowering: the cheap plastic decorations and the lateness of the day and the weird unappetizing candy fruit pieces in the fruitcake staring up at her from her fork. And emptiness. That was the worst of all the overpowering things.

"You really don't have to eat that if the mere idea of it's turning your stomach."

Angela shook her head, realizing her face must have twisted up in utter melancholy. "No, I—" and then a thought came to her. "I'm so far behind!" She smiled. "My sister's coming for Christmas, like she always does. Just the two of us. And it's my year to get the tree, and I've been trying to find one of those tree farms, and I know she's probably already made me ten presents, and I haven't gotten out to the store yet…" The lie felt so good to Angela that she just kept telling it.

"Let me buy two more little loaves," Angela insisted. "I swear, Gail loves this stuff."

Cyndi's smile was getting a little forced, but she sold Angela the loaves and wished her a happy holiday. She waved goodbye as the bells on the front door clunked—almost a *good riddance*, it seemed for a moment.

But Angela couldn't be bothered much by what the cashier thought of her odd, overly animated exit.

She was too anxious to get back on the road, zipping

through the handful of miles between herself and Sullivan, the last place her sister had ever called home.

***

The square had aged badly. Angela didn't recognize the few businesses still open. A flea market. A gas station with a couple of scraggly trees leaning against each other in the parking lot. A lonely old bookshop that had clearly already seen its best days. Only the medical building and the Bank of Sullivan remained familiar.

That bank—it loomed in a stately way, almost like a grandfather clock marking the time as it ticked by. Like it knew days gone by and Angela both.

She shivered. It was just a building, she had to remind herself. And scurried along, passing empty storefronts. "For Lease" signs were everywhere.

The uncomfortable feeling of having made a mistake found her again.

Christmas was not supposed to be so sad. Christmas, she thought, was supposed to feel like—well, it was supposed to feel like it did when she and Aunt Elizabeth visited Ruby's Place.

The hint of a smile crinkled her face. It had become a yearly thing for her and her beloved aunt. Both of them dressed in their newest and fanciest. Those special nights had made it seem as though the best of life could be crammed into a gift box and festooned with a ribbon.

Angela adjusted her itchy hat. That first year, she remembered, the only way she'd been able to go was by pretending that her Christmas Eve with Elizabeth was a "no sisters allowed" night. *That* was why she was the only one getting into Aunt Elizabeth's shiny Lincoln.

It made her sister's absence seem smaller.

But the truth had been far better than Angela's little daydream. Extraordinary, even. Because there for a while, a stretch of—what had it been, six, seven years?—she and Gail had shared part of their Christmas Eves in the back corner of Ruby's Place.

As Angela stood remembering, goosebumps danced down the back of her neck.

Chapter 6.

Angela's mind pinballed backward. She was thirteen, she remembered, and it was her sixth Christmas Eve meeting up with Gail at Ruby's. She carried her tray—filled with two cups of cocoa and two saucers piled high with marshmallows—to a table for two in the back corner. All around her, revelers were shouting, hugging, dancing, singing. A sequin-clad Evie pounded away at the piano while Dorothy continued to belt familiar carols. Children were propped on shoulders, clapping and singing along.

Angela walked with her elbows out, forcing the crowds away, protecting her tray from unintended bumps.

"Only dribbled a little bit," she said, placing a cup on the opposite side of the table. "Still got a full cup for you."

Gail appeared, filling the empty seat. She pushed up the sleeves of her red cable-knit sweater as she reached for the cocoa. Her dark curly hair hung only to the edge of her jawline—it had always been Angela's favorite of all Gail's hairdos. It pleased her to see it on her sister every year, the same way it pleased two best friends to find they liked the same kind of ice cream or the same band or the same movie—one more thing they had in common, one more reason they were close.

Angela pushed the tray aside and sat, smiling at her sister.

"You're different," Gail said, cocking her head to the side.

Angela frowned.

"I don't mean it in a bad way. You're just—growing up." Her eyes grew wistful as they bounced across Angela's face.

Angela felt anything but grown-up. But she was also far from being the seven-year-old in the floppy brown knit hat who had first shared Christmas meetings with her sister.

"I got bangs cut," Angela said with a shrug. She waited, wanting Gail to say something funny. Gail's soft, quiet way was making her nervous. Why wasn't she giggling, leaning forward, propping her chin on her hand and listening as Angela told her the stories of what had happened to her throughout the year?

"It's not the bangs," Gail said. After a pause, she added, "Before long, you know, you'll be older than me."

Angela flinched. It was kind of an awful thing to think about, frankly. Why would Gail bring it up on the one night of the year they had together?

"You pierced your ears," Gail said.

"Mom let me—"

"She made me wait until I was sixteen."

Angela knew what else she was looking at. "It's just a little lip gloss."

Gail offered a smile that only thinly covered up a hurt. The kind of smile you gave when you bumped into a former friend you'd fallen out of favor with.

"I look forward to these visits all year," Gail admitted. "But I want you to know, Angela, that it's okay."

"What's okay?"

"It's okay if you don't come."

"Why wouldn't I come?" Angela placed a hand on her chest, feeling wounded.

"I *want* you to change. I want you to wear earrings and makeup and cut your hair and meet new friends and fall in love and—" Gail leaned across the table. "Angela. Listen to me. I want you to forget me."

Angela gasped. "Why would I—"

Gail waved her hands. "I don't mean forever. I don't mean I want you to scrub me completely from your life. I'm saying—look, time goes on. And I'm not part of that. I'm not part of time anymore. Time left me behind. But the clock is still ticking for you. Changing you. Like it should. I'm frozen. You're not. And *I don't want you to be*. I don't want you to be stuck on me and what happened when you were seven. Do you understand what I'm trying to say?"

Angela shook her head.

"I'm saying there will be a time when you become so busy—with dating and parties and going to college and studying and working toward becoming *you*—that you won't remember to meet up with me. I'll slip your mind. You and Elizabeth will come here, and you'll maybe start singing with everybody, or you'll get to talking with Scott Drummond—"

71

"Scott Drummond!"

"One of these days," Gail warned her, "there will be a boy. Or a hundred other important things. And I'm telling you, one year, you will come here for Christmas Eve and forget to come to this table. And that's okay."

"I would never—"

"I've been expecting it."

"*Why?*"

"Because, Angie, that's the way it goes. It doesn't diminish anything between us. But you'll have so much to carry, so many new things, you'll have to put something down. *Just for a minute*, you'll think. You'll put me down, and I'll drift away. I'm asking you not to feel guilty about that. Don't you think twice about it. Okay?"

Angela felt horrified. Her mouth moved, but she could find no words to properly explain how she felt.

Gail smiled and began to speak in a happier tone, now that she had gotten that off her chest. "Tell me about school," she said, picking up her cup. "You get Mr. Scruggs for science?"

Angela tried to smile back, but faltered. "Yeah," she said. "Yeah, I did."

"Did he do that thing yet where he knows everybody's drifting off and he lets his voice get really, really soft, then… *bah!*" Gail shouted and threw her hands into Angela's face.

That time, Angela's smile grew stronger. "He did that exactly! Scared the whole class. And once…"

They fell back into the familiar rhythm of their yearly chat, their words glittering like holiday confetti against the air.

Chapter 7.

A ngela's fifty-two-year-old body shivered against the ancient memory of the last time she had ever seen Gail.

"It's over, Angela," she muttered to herself. "She's gone. Every bit as gone as Ruby's."

She'd just taken a step away when a cardinal flew straight at her. Before Angela could get her hands up to adequately protect herself, the cardinal whacked into her head, knocking Gail's ugly brown hat to the ground.

Angela scrambled to snatch the hat back up before it was stepped on or kicked to the side.

The square seemed oddly busy for that time of night, considering how few stores were left. None of the people on the sidewalk paused to so much as recognize her existence. And that made her feel not just lonely but invisible.

She picked up her hat and tried to return to the story she had fabricated back at the gas station—the one about her sister coming for Christmas. Yes, she tried to tell herself, she needed a tree and decorations...so much to get done before Gail's arrival. She tried picturing a life that Gail had always been part of. A life of regular phone calls and emails. She even tried imagining the visit not as something special, but humdrum. Something that had happened every single winter of her adult life. She probably would have even, some years, felt it was a chore. But no matter how she tried to think of it, the fantasy was hard to get back into, like trying to fall back into the same dream after waking.

She slammed the hat back on, but her feet wouldn't move. As she placed a hand on the flaking paint on the front door, and tilted her head back to get a good look at the crooked, broken neon sign, it came to her, the awful, selfish truth: She had stopped visiting Gail. So many important people and places and traditions had drifted from Angela's life as her teenage years appeared. Aunt Elizabeth. Coming to Ruby's every single year. But leaving her sister behind topped the unforgivable list. Why had she done it? And what did it matter that Gail herself had given her the okay—no, no, *encouraged* her—not to return for their Christmas meetings? Why would Angela listen? Why would she treat their magical moments together like nothing more than waving hello to a neighbor from the curb?

And now, here, at the point in her life when Angela would have liked nothing more than to see Gail again, there was no hope for it. Ruby's was closed. Gail was gone forever.

Angela was still standing quietly, hands in her coat pockets, when someone slammed into her, knocking her into the door. Her shoulder and head whacked painfully against the wood—so hard, a few green paint chips flaked off onto her coat.

Angela turned, ready to bark something at the man who had so rudely smashed her into the door. But he was already nearly at the end of the street, ready to turn at the intersection.

She hadn't seen anybody move that fast since—well, since she'd gone to watch her sister's track meets. It had seemed to Angela back then that the girl could absolutely fly. So many memories bubbled up around her. They were lovely. And they hurt, too.

Perched on the nearby street sign, the cardinal flapped its wings at Angela.

"Cardinals appear when angels are near," she recited, before stopping short to offer a quick disbelieving snort. "Not that there are any angels around this place. Not anymore. If there ever were to begin with—" she tried to add, as though to convince herself it hadn't *really* been all that special after all. Gail hadn't really been there at Ruby's. In her grief, Angela had simply been susceptible to Dorothy's story. And then, when her grief was no longer crushing her, she made up that last encounter with Gail.

"Of course I did," Angela told herself. "I made it up…"

Her words trailed as other voices came to her.

But from where? Ruby's Place looked like it had been closed for years—even the "For Sale or Lease" sign was sun-bleached and dirty and a bit rough around the edges, the paper eaten by moths, maybe. The sidewalk had completely emptied. The "Closed" signs were suddenly all turned to face the street.

Ruby's padlock, Angela noted, was busted. Had that

happened when she'd hit the door? The entrance was slightly ajar. And—was that light trickling from the doorway? Was music playing—live music from a piano? Was a crowd singing, their voices sounding far stronger than that silly old Alvin and the Chipmunks song she'd just heard at the gas station?

Angela inched closer, pushing the door open.

At that moment, Ruby's exploded all around her. The room bustled with excitement. Here it all was, just as she had stored it away in her memory. The crowd and the singing and the candles and the smell of pine. Ladies in silk and satin, men with hats in hand, and the melding aromas of cologne and snow and chimney smoke brought in from the outside. The pinstriped suits and the heels with rhinestone clips.

Oh, it was so lovely. Angela's eyes tingled; a warmth overtook her.

She bumped and bobbed and weaved through the crowd, all the way to the bar.

"Hot cocoa," the bartender said with a wink. "Extra plate of marshmallows on the side."

"O—okay," Angela muttered, unsure why the bartender would act as though she'd memorized Angela's preferred treat.

"One holiday special comin' up," she said, turning to whip up her order.

"When did you reopen?" Angela bellowed over the laughter and the shouts and the piano chords.

The woman behind the bar looked remarkably like the owner she remembered. Same slender body. And she seemed to prefer the same well-placed bun at the back of her head. But the bun was brown, instead of the silver Angela had known Ruby to wear.

The resemblance was striking. Surely this woman had to be a family member. "Did you inherit the place from Ruby?" Angela asked.

The crowd continued to belt "Up on the Housetop" as the bartender slid the mug and a small saucer of marshmallows in front of her.

Angela stared at the marshmallows, memories pummeling her again. "Just like Ruby used to make," she muttered. They had that imperfect look about them, unlike store-bought marshmallows. Toasted on top. She took a sip of the cocoa and moaned in pleasure—something she hadn't done in ages. When she took a bite of the marshmallows, they tasted of winters and warmth and the closeness of friends. They tasted like the love she had held for her aunt. They tasted like hope and the feeling of being able to step into a future full of possibility. Of being at the beginning of things, rather than the end. Wasn't that really how she'd felt in Ruby's? That she'd never really lost anything? That as long as she was there, she never could?

Before Angela swallowed the sweets, Ruby poured a flute of champagne. As the bubbles traveled toward the top of the glass, the barstool beside Angela jiggled.

And there she sat: Aunt Elizabeth herself.

Angela couldn't catch her breath.

She glanced about, taking in the faces of the revelers once again. And realized, as the blood ran from her face, that she recognized these people. There was Evie, pounding the ivories like she had when Angela was little. The man at the grocery store who had given her a fresh sugar cookie each time she'd shown up with her mother. The Shoemakers, her childhood neighbors. The librarian from her elementary school. And was that—the singer, leaning against the piano. Wasn't that Dorothy? Wonderful, sweet, magical Dorothy, who had told Angela the story of Chester? Who had opened her up to the possibility of seeing Gail? Each one of them looking young and vibrant and wearing fashions from bygone eras.

Could it be? Was it possible? They were all still here? Frozen in time?

Was Gail—could she be? Behind Angela, the table in the corner remained empty.

"Who are you looking for, dear?" Elizabeth asked.

"I—I—" Angela's eyes darted back toward the mirror behind the bar. There she was, in that awful brown hat. Sitting next to her aunt, who looked as glamorous as ever.

She snatched the hat off her head and tossed it onto the counter just as the bartender's face filled the mirror. "Ruby," she muttered, finally recognizing her.

"Get you something else, Angela?" Ruby asked.

Angela laughed nervously. "It really is you," she whispered.

"Who else would it be?" Ruby asked. "Nobody can run this place like me."

Angela's head spun. "You're all here. How—"

As though to answer, Ruby quickly poured a scotch neat, scooted it across the bar. Walter Drummond from the bank appeared beside the drink, still wearing one of his favorite wide-collared pinstriped suits. Just as Elizabeth had appeared next to her champagne.

"Where's—your son? Where's Scott?" Angela asked. It would be lovely to see her old classmate.

"He's not part of this," Walter said, with the kind of gruff tone that declared the question was absurd.

"Why not? He was always here," Angela protested.

"He runs the bank now," Walter said.

"But he could still—" Angela started.

Walter shook his head.

Winter hit Angela's bloodstream. She shivered. "It's true, then. Everyone here is a—well. You—" she stammered. "This is so strange. I was just feeling like—"

"—like you had the old Christmas spirit again?" Elizabeth finished, taking a sip of the champagne Ruby had prepared for her.

Walter stood. "To Christmas spirits, who are all still alive and well!" he bellowed.

The room erupted in cheers. Glasses were lifted.

"Yes," Ruby told her, "the ghosts of Christmases past are all still here."

She poured a margarita, and a woman appeared in a white blouse (complete with circa 1986 shoulder pads) that offered the perfect contrast to her black mane and dark skin. "Barbara Lewis," she introduced herself to Angela. Then shouted it again when she didn't think Angela heard over the din. "This place could wake the dead," she said with a wink.

She took a sip of her drink and nodded. "Not bad," she told Ruby.

"Not bad?" Walter echoed. "Nobody mixes a drink like old Rubes." Walter and Barbara elbowed each other, pleased with the joke.

"Is that—that's how they show up?" Angela asked, pointing to the margarita glass Barbara carried off with her. "You mix a favorite drink and they appear?"

Angela began to tremble. It was all still here. Nothing had aged. Not in Ruby's Place. Her heart swelled. If that was true, she thought, then hope was also still alive, it was still inside her, just waiting for a nudge.

Everything came back to her. All those things she thought she'd lost. The warmth of Christmas. The closeness of Aunt Elizabeth. She hadn't realized how much the memory of their time together had begun to fade. Now that all the details were fresh again, now that she was hearing Elizabeth's voice and smelling her perfume, she realized how foggy she'd let these memories become.

It was wrong to get so mired in her own bad feelings that she'd forgotten the bright, wonderful specialness of it all.

"Fewer and fewer people are coming in each year," Ruby observed softly.

"Fewer and fewer remember Ruby's fondly," Elizabeth agreed, sadness lacing her tone. "Fewer and fewer are left who have memories that beg revisiting."

"What—what does that mean?" Angela asked.

Before she could fully get her grips on it all, Aunt Elizabeth had her hand under her arm and was hoisting her off the stool, like she had when she was little. She was steering her through the door and onto the sidewalk.

"Wait—wait—it can't be over, can it?" Angela asked.

She swiveled, but the padlock was back on the door.

She raced to the front window and peered inside.

The place was empty. It looked as though it had been empty for ages.

Angela touched the bump on her forehead that had begun to rise from the spot where she'd whacked her head against the door.

Who had that been, the person who had pushed her into the door? How *had* she broken the padlock?

Then again, had she broken it? Had she hit her head harder than she'd thought? Was her heart emptier than she'd thought? Had she simply needed to see someone other than a random woman in a gas station, one who was offering her dry fruitcake and making her come up with some silly story about her sister? Had she imagined Ruby's Place coming back to life?

She sighed, started to turn away.

And stopped when she saw it. There it was. Her hat. On the bar.

She *had* been inside.

Angela trembled.

"What—" she blubbered. "What—"

"Cheer, cheer, cheer," she heard. When she glanced up, she saw the cardinal was back, flapping his wings near the entrance.

He fluttered away, around the edge of the building.

Angela followed.

Wasn't there a back step? In an alley? Wasn't that where Dorothy had told her the story of Chester when Angela was small?

She walked with purpose, thinking how unfamiliar the alley now looked. The door had literally been nailed shut. "No Trespassing!" signs snarled.

But Angela wasn't about to let this go. She grabbed a brick and hurled it at the door.

The door didn't budge.

She picked up the brick a second time.

"I believe," Angela insisted. Then, to everyone and no one in particular, she shouted, "Do you hear me? I believe!"

The insistent cardinal swooped around Angela's face and zipped straight toward the door. Instead of crashing against it, the bird aimed straight for one of the old bullet holes, the leftover scar from a long-ago Christmas Eve raid.

He flew straight into the hole, disappearing into the building.

Angela dropped the brick and squatted to get a closer look. "No way could he have fit in that thing," Angela muttered. But there it was, at the edge of the bullet hole:

A red feather.

As Angela spun it between her frozen thumb and index finger, the door banged open.

"Ga—?" she started.

Her sister wasn't there.

But her aunt was. And Ruby.

And the smell of marshmallows.

And a cardinal, who fluttered out of the now open doorway, into the night sky.

"And you dared bet against me, Ruby," Elizabeth muttered. "I told you she'd be back. No kicking her out would keep her gone too long. This place is important to her. We can trust her. We always did."

Angela straightened up, stars glittering as they once had when she was young. Suddenly, she knew what she wanted for Christmas.

A funny thing about those Christmas lists, Angela learned that year—turns out, wanting something isn't completely selfish. It's not always just about *stuff*. It means you have hope that good things are soon to come your way.

It means no matter your age, you have a dream.

Chapter 8.

The very next best chapter in Angela's always story occurred one year later, during another Christmas Eve in Sullivan.

But it wasn't really a *next* Christmas, not for Angela. It was her *first*—as the brand-new owner of Ruby's Place.

And, to her great satisfaction, the facilitator of hundreds of other always stories.

She had restored Ruby's Place—fixed the neon sign and polished the hardwood floors. She had rescued the original furniture from storage and spruced up the old carved bar itself, which had looked even to a young Angela like an ornate jewelry box or a cedar box of keepsakes.

Elizabeth and Ruby and Dorothy and Walter—familiar ghosts of Christmases past—were all there, too. As were so many other such spirits. It had become a nightly occurrence, all of them appearing once Angela had turned the "Closed" sign and Ruby had begun to mix favorite drinks. An after-hours happy hour, populated by guests Angela had simply come to think of as regulars.

On Christmas Eve, the regulars came early. Before

closing. And they brought along additional faces from yesterday. Yes, at Ruby's Place, the "spirits" referred to far more than just the bottles behind the bar. On Christmas Eve, they circled through the crowd, tapping the shoulders of current Sullivan residents, sliding into chairs, laughing at the shocked reactions of husbands and parents and friends and siblings.

This was the gift that was Ruby's Place. One last moment for customers to connect with a special someone. The someone who had become merely a name in the obituaries, a newspaper clipping folded and yellowing in a scrapbook. Someone believed by the outside world to exist only in photos, in hazy remembrances, remaining forever frozen at one point in time, never growing older.

It was what had driven Angela through months of hard work and setbacks, through blown budgets and readjusted estimates. She was going to make sure the people of Sullivan had a chance to experience the same gift that Dorothy had shown her she would find there.

It was a gift to herself, as well. To see her own Sullivan neighbors leaning over tables, tears filling their eyes as that one person—the missing piece of their own heart—finally got a chance to hear everything that had been left unspoken. *I love you* or *I miss you* or *I'm sorry.*

That night, as the meetings filled the air, every bit as sweet as the smell of marshmallows, Angela poured three champagnes. And she, Ruby, and Elizabeth toasted their triumph.

Angela smiled, but she wasn't exactly through dreaming. Not yet. One wish still had not yet been granted.

"This isn't what I expected at all," Scott Drummond, current bank manager, confessed midway through the evening, sliding onto a just-vacated barstool.

"Why not? It's just like Ruby's old place," Angela said, placing her own glass of champagne beneath the bar. "Told you it would be, back when I came for the loan. Did you forget what it looked like? You were always here with your dad on Christmas Eve."

Scott held Angela's eyes for a moment. "But you—when you came to me for the loan, at the bank, you knew it was more. Didn't you?"

Angela stared back at him, unsure how to respond. Scott had seen his dad. He'd seen Walter. She was certain of it.

"You knew how special it was," he pressed. "Didn't you? In a way I didn't."

Angela stiffened. "The past feels close in here," she said, choosing her words carefully. In a town that loved its gossip, she would forever walk a tightrope. *Something mysterious in there* or *just can't describe it* would help bring the curious out. But *the place is filled with spirits—and you can talk with the person you miss the most* would mean that the building would be inundated. Overwhelmed. Perhaps in a way that would make the regulars skitter off for good.

Nobody wanted to be the oddity, ogled by onlookers.

"You bring the rest of the family?" Angela asked.

Scott nodded. "My kids and wife and—" he turned, nearly slipping off the stool. "I think—I had one too many cups of your punch. My wife'll be driving home, clearly."

Angela grinned inwardly. That, too, was part of the

plan. Surely, those who were lucky enough to reconnect with the faces of the past would share many of the same questions: *Was I caught up in the holiday? Did I just have too many red wines?*

When they returned the next year, their loved one would not appear. A single meeting, no more. She and the regulars had agreed on as much, at Ruby's insistence. Mystery. It was all about maintaining mystery. They trusted what Ruby said. She'd spent half her life in the footlights, after all. She knew all about drawing—or keeping—just the right amount of a crowd.

And yet, there was a piece of this night that would always remain, in Scott and in everyone else who'd had a similar experience. Reopening Ruby's Place, Angela knew, was the same as the reopening of a heart.

"How about a coffee?" Angela asked, pouring him a cup. "Take the kids some of my fudge?"

"Sounds great," he said, pushing himself to his feet. "And Angela?"

"Yeah?" Her stomach knotted.

"Thanks. For this place." He wagged a finger at her. "I should have known," he said. "You and that memory of yours. You remember everything. I should have known it would be the same down to the last *detail*. Feel like I just left my dad at a table back there ten *minutes* ago. How could I feel that way?" He was still searching for some sort of confirmation.

She reached across the bar to squeeze Scott's hand.

"It's you, Angela," he slurred. "It's all because of you."

"Go on," she said. "Go back to your family. I can bring

the treats to your table."

The celebration carried on for hours. Well past midnight. Some of her customers—Scott included—attempted to return to the building after closing. Vying for one last look now that they were sober. But the regulars had already declared the evening a success, Walter had gathered up the deposits for the night, and they had all vanished from the premises. Nothing to see. Nothing to prove. Scott and the others simply dragged themselves away, each of them feeling a nagging sense of wonder.

Angela filled a tray with two cups of cocoa and extra marshmallows. Sweat broke out, like she'd suddenly been thrust into a hundred degree day. She locked her elbows against her sides to keep the cups from trembling off.

She made her way across the bar, passing the pine boughs on each table, soaking in the still-flickering candlelight, smiling at the warm red ribbons on all the sconces and the backs of chairs.

Her breath came in quick pants as she placed her tray on a table for two in the back.

She tugged the old hat from her pocket. The brown one. And plopped into her seat.

Moments ticked by.

The cocoa grew cold.

The marshmallows colder.

Perhaps, Angela thought, it was simply too quiet in Ruby's Place. Maybe it didn't sound welcoming. Maybe it sounded empty—like Angela wasn't even there. Desperate, she took a deep breath and squeaked the opening line of "It's

Beginning to Look a Lot Like Christmas." Somehow, though, it sounded thin and sad.

And still, she sat.

Until disappointment began to creep in, a tide growing ever closer.

"I did this for you, Gail," she murmured. "So you would come back. So we could see each other again."

But Gail did not appear.

The tide of disappointment washed over Angela, swallowing her whole.

Reality Strikes Again...

Geena

That was as far as I got.

I placed the laptop down on the coffee table, finally prying my fingers from the keys.

I felt limp and spent after writing such a large swath of Angela's always story—like I'd just run about fifty miles. My legs wobbled beneath me when I got up to answer the old landline. "Merry Christmas, babe," Rob said. "Although—it's almost the day after Christmas by now."

"Are you serious?" I checked the clock. "Is that a p.m. time?" I peeled the curtains back in the living room to check out the sky above the backyard. Pitch black.

"What's going on over there, anyway?" he asked. "This is the fourth time I've called."

"Fourth?" I hadn't even heard the phone ring.

"Yeah—tried to get you over here for some cinnamon rolls and bacon this morning. Then an afternoon walk. Then dinner. If you hadn't answered this time, I was going to drive out there. Make sure you were okay."

"I was just—involved in a book," I murmured, staring

at my laptop.

"Mmmm," he'd said. "Reminds me of our reading dates. When we were kids. Remember?"

Did I. Our reading dates were somewhat legendary in Sullivan. Not that anyone believed they were reading dates.

Parked out there at the edge of town for hours, people used to whisper.

She'll be pregnant by the spring.

Yes, so sad. She has so much potential, that Geena.

We always laughed when we overheard their whispers. Little did they know we started out at The Page Turner, where Rob would buy some sci-fi horror paperback, and I'd wind up with what he usually called "some Jane Eyre thing," and we'd curl up in that giant Caprice of his, and just read, me with my head on his chest, listening to his heart and the soft turn of pages.

"Those were always my favorites," I agreed.

He chuckled. "The special bond of book junkies."

But he had no inkling that the book I was absorbed in was my own.

I was still staring at my laptop, remembering all the furious typing I'd done. Racing to get the images I'd seen outside of Ruby's down on paper. Or down on screen, at least. Eight chapters. When previously, I'd had none.

Were they as good as I'd felt they were when I'd written them? My eyes burned. My back ached.

"Sure you're okay?" Rob asked.

"Yeah," I said. "Yeah—perfect."

"Coming to the store tomorrow?"

"Wouldn't miss it. I'll even take you and Justin out to dinner."

I hung up, wandering back toward the sofa. "Eight chapters," I muttered through a smile.

I had a brief moment of dread. For the first time since I'd started typing, I didn't know what the first line of the next chapter would be.

But I also hadn't slept since the night before last.

Without turning my laptop off, I simply stacked the microwave pizza containers and cereal bowls on the floor, to be gathered up later. Who could bother with cleaning up when a book—a real, live book, *my book, finally*—was leaping out of my fingers? I just needed a few hours of sleep. Then I could get back to it. More chapters. More scenes.

My eyes began to droop. I had eight solid chapters. I kept repeating it in my mind: eight chapters.

I felt sure, right then, that nine and beyond would write just as quickly. Chapter eight was as far as I'd gotten right then. But it wasn't as far as I'd ever get.

Back at Ruby's Place

Now that the last few hours of Christmas were officially sliding away under the dark of night, Walter reappeared inside Ruby's Place. He had a job to do—collect the nightly deposits.

Angela hadn't opened at all on Christmas Day. Even the after-hours regulars had skipped their happy hour that night. Christmas Eve was exhausting for everyone involved. A full day was necessary to let everything that had happened sink in. To cool off. Walter was the only one who had returned. He was the banker, after all. Even now.

He carefully counted it—twice, just to be sure—and placed the stack of holiday deposits in a zippered envelope, which he then slipped into his coat. He turned off the lights, heading toward the Bank of Sullivan.

By the time he found himself on the sidewalk, night was fading. The sky had begun to broadcast the earliest streaks of dawn. It was, officially, the day after Christmas.

Another Christmas season had come to an end.

Walter took a deep breath. The world had a different

smell after Christmas. Warmer, it seemed. At least for a little while.

Especially this one. For the second year in a row, he had seen his son—his Scott, no longer little Scotty. Last year, they had talked. About Saturday mornings. And Little League. And fishing. And sledding in the winter. And all those *don't tell your mother* adventures of theirs. This year, Scott had returned to the bar, glancing about, hopeful. Walter had stepped up behind his son, placed a hand on his shoulder. He'd felt Scott relax beneath his touch. Saw his face shift in the mirror behind the bar. Scott had not seen or heard Walter, a rule established by the regulars: only one Christmas Eve visit allowed. But Walter's presence had still given Scott a sense of comfort—that much was obvious. And that had filled Walter with gladness.

Now, Walter whistled, invigorated, his breath drawing cloudy confessions in the night sky. He had seen his son.

He slipped inside the Bank of Sullivan, slowly making his way across the marble floor. Desks supported computer screens instead of the typewriters Walter had known, but the work was the same—as tedious at times as it was important.

He veered toward the cleanest desk of all; so clean, in fact, that had he not known better, he might have assumed whoever worked at this particular station had only just been hired. No time yet for clutter. In reality, it belonged to his son. Scott Drummond, the bank's current general manager, whose penchant for neatness was one of the few items left out for display. He'd always been that way, even as a boy. His model airplanes had never had a single glob of glue running down their sides. Albums had always been in the right sleeves. Jackets hung in his closet, each on its own wooden hanger, all of them facing the same direction.

Walter took enormous pride in the fact that one of the few framed pictures Scott had placed on the corner of the desk—the same desk Walter had once called his own—was of himself. His hand on the shoulder of a young Scott, the two of them wearing nearly identical three-piece suits. Red rose boutonnieres. While standing in front of a fireplace decked out with tinsel and pine.

They were on their way to Ruby's Place, as they always were on Christmas Eve. Walter had believed back then that with so many voices laughing and shouting—the carols, the gifts, the marshmallows and magic—young Scott wouldn't have to think about his parents' divorce. Or the fact that the holiday had a split down the middle of it, half for Mom, half for Dad. It didn't matter that Scott would be picked up first thing on Christmas Day, by a step-father who remained something of a stranger. Christmas Eve blocked all that out. It was their own time. A whole evening that belonged to Walter and Scott, one that no one else could barge in on.

Walter removed his hat, placing it on Scott's desk. He picked up the photo of the two of them, nestled in the midst of school pictures of Scott's children, photos of the family dog, Goldie, and a vacation shot of Scott and his wife in a tropical location. Walter's slightly yellow, fading image offered additional proof that those nights had been as special to Scott as they had been to Walter. An always story to be shared with Scott's own children.

He smiled and began to sing "Silver Bells" as he slipped past the current vault, to the back of the bank. His voice sounded great in the empty building—the notes bounced about joyfully.

Until he found himself standing in front of it. Yes, there it was, in its ancient, half-tarnished glory: the old original vault, no longer in use.

Well. No longer in present-tense use, anyway.

Which made it the perfect place to put the night's deposits.

Because these deposits didn't have anything to do with money. They were the memories that had swirled through the air in Ruby's Place on Christmas Eve. Now, here, he could store them in Sullivan's Memory Bank.

Walter whirled the combination lock. He took a deep breath and tightened his mouth. It required every ounce of his strength to swing the old door open.

Inside, he found a large safe deposit box. He cracked it open and placed the night's deposits inside.

For safekeeping. Until next year.

Geena
A Year in My Life

I'd love to say I woke up and returned to my book. I'd love to say that over the next week—even two—I pounded out a full draft. But the truth was, I couldn't figure out what to do with the next chapter, let alone the rest of the story.

I'd seen more than what I'd written. The full history of Ruby's Place. I saw the building before it even belonged to Ruby. The speakeasy days and Frankie. Dorothy the singer. The same Dorothy who'd told Angela that story about seeing Chester inside Ruby's. All those decades. All that time. But how did that weave in with Angela's story? Should it?

It certainly seemed so, especially considering the fact that Angela's tale intertwined with Dorothy's. I had seen *all* of Dorothy's story. Heard her voice. Saw her cloche hat and her ivory gown. Saw that nothing had been right for her until that old trumpet of Chester's had walked into the It Ain't Over Yet. Just weeks before I'd discovered the old bottle in the snow, Tina had put Chester's trumpet on display in the front window. It was a distinctive looking instrument, custom-made, with vines and flowers carved all over it. With its white metal skin glimmering in the sunlight, Chester had finally appeared. He had not been able to return to town—or to Dorothy—without that trumpet. They were not the same without their music, after all.

That very Christmas Eve, Dorothy's dream had come true. Chester had come back to her. Their melodies filled Ruby's just as they had once Frankie's speakeasy, like the most spectacular of Christmas miracles.

An always story for the ages.

An always story that might not have ever been possible without Angela and the reopening of the bar.

But what did it all mean?

I wasn't sure of anything anymore. Not about where to go with the book, and not even about what I'd already written. Did Angela ever see Gail? Why didn't I know that? Why hadn't I seen it? Come to think of it, why had my visions of Sullivan ended before the Christmas Eve I'd found the bottle? Why would the liquor show me a story without an end?

Maybe I'd gotten it all wrong. Maybe the focus never should have been on Angela. Maybe I'd missed the bigger picture, and those eight chapters were nothing but a long-winded mistake.

Maybe, I even thought (mostly out of desperation), I could get a new vision to appear by trying out new possibilities. Maybe, if I was onto something, another white flash would engulf me and I'd see it all play out, the entire ending.

Brainstorming brought a full trash can. I hoped sleeping on it would fix my problem—but night after night, I simply tossed and turned. A few days after Christmas, I had Rob over; we watched some of my home movies and talked about old times and once he was gone, I returned to my book. Or tried to. Yet again. Even took a couple of sips from the remnants sloshing around in the bottom of the antique bottle I'd taken for my own. The rancid taste left me gagging—but with no additional scenes to witness and then transcribe, as had happened with my previous chapters. All I saw was what I had already seen. What I had already written. No new understanding of the role Ruby's had played in Sullivan. No new revelation about the people who populated my pages. No new guidance on how to incorporate some of the town's additional history, those scenes I had left out.

Nothing.

I had nothing.

Not even an upset stomach from that putrid old liquor.

A cardinal landed on my windowsill and began to peck out a repeating rhythm, over and over. I wanted to pound out my own S.O.S., to whomever the patron saint of storytellers was.

And still. Nothing.

As the days pressed on, it became clear that wasn't changing.

I had no idea how to finish my book.

With a heavy heart, I slipped my printed pages into the top drawer of Dad's old writing desk—the same one he'd used to pay our bills or address Christmas cards. And I texted the head of the University of Iowa English Department, apologizing for the delay in my response. I gave him some line about how I'd been consumed with the last few difficult-to-resolve issues regarding my father's estate. And—can you believe it?—my cell had broken in the midst of it! I added that one for good measure. Maybe he saw through it. Scratch that. He definitely saw through it. But it was the holidays, the one time of year when shenanigans and half-truths could be quietly overlooked.

At the end of my winter break, I kissed Rob goodbye, saying I'd be back when the daffodils bloomed. Locked up the house. And headed back to Iowa. I fell into the rhythm of classes and grading. As promised, I came back to Rob and Sullivan during spring break and after summer school wrapped. There was another rhythm about being home, one I could quickly fall back into again: the easy beat of Rob and I wandering through hot days and humid nights. Beers shared with the fireflies. We split the upkeep of two houses, mowing the lawns and painting the porches. He helped me install a new whole-house fan. I helped him hang new curtains. Before I knew it, I'd swallowed up this enormous gob of time, and suddenly, I was back in sweaters and gloves and kicking snow from my boots before heading into the English building. Fall semester was winding down. Christmas was coming back around.

And I was thinking again about the book I'd crammed in a drawer in my childhood home, the pages now a year old.

Chris Baxter, former journalist turned composition and rhetoric instructor, was the only one who knew how preoccupied I'd become—even if he couldn't exactly be sure why. We shared an office, after all, and it was hard to keep too many secrets from somebody who practically sat in your lap all day. I knew a few of his, like the fact that he was back to the cigarettes he'd sworn he'd given up thirteen years ago. Didn't matter how many peppermints he tried to cram into his mouth after sneaking a smoke.

"When're you going back?" he asked. It was getting to be that draggy part of the semester when everybody existed on caffeine and bad food—even the instructors. Eyes were bloodshot, clothes were rumpled and stained. Everybody reeked of stale coffee and the fumes they were running on. Too many chapters to cram into the last few class periods, too many term papers to read.

"Soon as I get final grades turned in." I leaned back in my office chair. I was pretty sure the thing had busted sometime around 1975, but it had broken in all the right places—for me, anyway. Only problem was, it squeaked. Every single time I crossed my legs or shifted my weight or exhaled. Chris had often cringed against the noise, saying he was going to toss the chair out the window, into the dumpster below—with me in it if I tried to stop him. One of those empty threats somebody uses on you as a running joke.

"Why don't you come too?" I asked.

"What—to Sullivan? With you?"

"Yeah. Why not?"

"Ahhhh," he groaned, clutching his chest. "Don't do that."

"Do what?"

"Take pity on the poor pitiful bachelor."

"I'm not."

He gave me a kind of *get real* look.

"You said you knew Sullivan," I justified.

"Knew *of* Sullivan. There's a difference."

"Explain yourself, professor. Be *specific*." I pointed a pen at him, like I was standing at the front of a classroom, demanding an in-depth explanation from the fourth-year student in the second row.

He rolled his eyes at me, his comeback straight to the point. "I have never actually been in town. I've been in the surrounding area. But not in town. Which means I don't have something sentimental there, calling me back."

"So this'll be your first year to *acquire* something sentimental," I countered, making sure my tone matched his.

"It's your home, not mine. And you'll want to spend your time with what's-his-name—"

"Rob," I finished. "I have so many extra rooms in that house, it's almost obscene for a single person to be in there all alone. Seriously. Rob's busy with the store, and it's not like we live together or anything—"

"Ooh, now there's a good topic. Let's talk about that. Why *aren't* there any wedding bells in your immediate future, *hmmmm*?"

"Because Rob's done the marriage thing. Because, as it turns out, I don't need a ring on my finger. Because the two of us spent nearly thirty years apart, then were able to fall right back into the old us. Because we know what makes us work as much as being together are the times we spend apart. Missing someone can actually feel good—when you know you'll get to see them again. Ever Google living apart together relationships?" I raised my eyebrow.

Chris grunted. He'd assumed that trying to dig into my own private life would have made me back off. He hadn't expected me to offer an honest answer so quickly.

"Well?" I asked. "You comin' or not?"

"Why do you want me to?"

"Because you're my friend. Because I enjoy your company. Really. I could use a friend to help make that house feel not so empty."

That much was true. The house felt awful without my dad in it. So much so, I had recently called the old home number. And when Dad's voice picked up on the machine, I'd said, "Hey, it's me. Just calling to let you know I'll be on the road as soon as I get my last grades turned in. See you soon."

A little bit of imagining. Just like Angela had done in my own pages. I had to admit, it really did feel good, making up a story about spending the holiday with Dad.

"I'm not all that into Christmas," he muttered.

I spit out a hearty laugh at that one. "Give me a break. You don't like Christmas, but you've got a decorated mini tree on your desk?"

Chris still had that twisted, tortured look on his face. The one that said he knew he was gearing up to be the odd wad, the third wheel, the guy with no other plans on a major holiday. "I've got so much to get done before the next semester—" he started.

"Workaholic," I teased.

"Kettle," he lobbed back, because we'd both been accused of the same thing. He'd already told me how much he hated the term, how misleading it was. *The way people say it,* he'd said, *it clinks. Sounds like an empty bottle hitting the trash. But it's not empty at all, is it? If it's the right work? It's fulfilling. It gives life shape and meaning.*

"You know you'd like to see it," I told him. "Ruby's Place on Christmas Eve, I mean. The way I've talked it up? You have to be curious."

His face changed then, like I'd revealed I knew something about him that I shouldn't.

He fidgeted, causing a small spiral notebook to poke out of his shirt pocket. As a collector of stories, Chris was never without that notebook. It was the first thing that had endeared him to me—the ice breaker, the reason we'd become friends. To begin with, we'd been assigned the office together by the department—two instructors with last names at the beginning of the alphabet. But it had been a strained kind of sharing at the start, the sort you do with strangers in public restrooms, pretending not to even notice the other person.

But I saw him around campus, talking everyone up: wayward freshmen and janitors and the guys who refilled the Pepsi machines. Department secretaries and librarians. As soon as the conversation was over—and the person he'd been talking to was out of sight—he'd write everything down in that little pocket notebook of his.

"What do you do with them, anyway?" I'd finally asked. The first words I'd ever said to him that wasn't, "Morning" or, "No problem" (usually in response to his drawer in the filing cabinet bumping into something of mine). I was sitting outside the English-Philosophy Building, trying to work up some lesson plan or another. And there he was, scribbling away after talking to one of the university landscapers. "Are you going to publish it?"

"Publish!" He said it like I'd suggested something utterly profane.

"That or perish, right?"

"I'd never dream of it. I'd gladly perish."

I'd laughed at the absurdity of the whole thing. He'd grinned, proudly. And we'd been friends ever since.

"Come *on*," I grumbled, nudging his knee with my foot. "If you're going to see Ruby's Place, you need to see it on Christmas. You don't want to have to hear me just blabber on about the place for a whole 'nother year. If we both go, I won't have to bore you by rehashing all the details." Even though I'd really only shared the most basic details of Sullivan, never once wading into the truth about the book I'd started after drinking from an old bottle I'd found sticking out of the snow outside Ruby's. Maybe, it occurred to me, it was part of why I wanted him to come. Maybe, deep down, I wanted to show him the pages.

"Besides," I added, pointing at his shirt pocket, deciding to use it to my advantage, "you'll get plenty of stories for that thing." But it wasn't just a ploy to get him to agree. I really did want to know what he'd see at the old bar—there was a distinct possibility that I hadn't seen the book's ending because it hadn't happened yet. Maybe it would play out that very Christmas, to be written in the same kind of flurry that

I'd written the beginning. I didn't want to miss it. I needed another set of eyes. Story collector eyes.

He chuckled, rubbing his face. He hadn't put his grading pen down first, though, and he made a little slashing mark on his face, right underneath the graying fringe of his hair and above a wicked looking scar that ran down his jawline. A sledding accident, he'd said. But not when he was a boy. When he was grown—one of the few stories I'd heard him tell of a woman in his life, the former love. The two of them on the same sled, tumbling down a hill one winter, like kids.

I knew it was possible I'd regret what I'd just offered. Work friends sometimes don't translate well to off-hours. And there was much the two of us didn't really know about each other. The secrets our shared space had uncovered were only the most benign. I knew his deeper details in the most vague way—a boyhood in the Midwest, the state never really specified. A romance in his twenties with a woman, never given so much as a name. I got the feeling, though, that it had been serious, that they'd come close to marrying. Sometimes, the cloudy vagueness he offered seemed purposefully secretive— like there'd been something about the whole thing he didn't want me to know. And here I was, inviting him into my home.

Still, though, I didn't want to take it back. I wanted him to come to Sullivan.

"Okay," he said. "I've got some things I need to get done around here, though, so—can we agree I'll be there, say, Christmas Eve?"

"Christmas Eve?" I bellowed. "Talk about cutting it close. If you come that late, you'll need to stay through the new year."

He laughed. "One holiday at a time. Don't rush me. Like I said, I've got plenty I have to do. With you gone, I might just finally have the perfect opportunity to get rid of that rotten chair."

"Fair enough," I laughed, and we shook on it.

The Memory Bank

Walter hiked his collar, protecting the back of his neck from a cold burst of night air. He straightened the brim of his hat, thinking it was a shame that no one wore hats anymore. Dress hats, not like that awful brown knit thing Angela wore. Hats like his could make the world feel special. Like it was a place worth dressing up for.

Yes, Walter thought, taking in the silver decorations and the glittering stars as he made his way down the sidewalk, it was the perfect night for his yearly withdrawal, the one he made in December as the holiday season appeared on the horizon.

He paused outside the Bank of Sullivan, recalling the years he had spent inside. All the long hours, the stacks of documents waiting for his signature, the endless telephone calls. Paper pusher—maybe that was all some folks figured being a banker amounted to. Walter had known better.

Decades ago, as the Vice President of the Bank of Sullivan, Walter had dealt in the future. That's what he'd told Scott. "Remember, son," he'd said, "that's not just money in the vault. It's hopes. Dreams. It's somebody's house where they'll raise their kids. It's a new business that will go into an empty space in one of those old buildings on the square. It's tomorrow—and the tomorrow after that."

These days, though, as the current keeper of Sullivan's always stories, Walter dealt in the past.

He slipped inside and made a beeline for the old vault. The former cornerstone of the bank, the relic of yesterday that no longer held money but something far more valuable. Every one of the always stories that had ever taken place at Ruby's was safely stored inside.

As he'd done before, Walter whirled the lock and grunted as he heaved that heavy old vault open.

He then carried a large safe deposit box to a nearby window. Balancing the box in one hand, he cranked the old casement window open with the other.

He lifted the box lid, slowly, his face scrunched up protectively. The memories, he knew from past experience, would flap their wings almost violently as they raced through the open window. They'd be anxious to fly, having been cooped up for months. Anxious to dance on the windowsills of Sullivan homes, to perch on the phone lines.

But tonight, when the safe deposit box opened, the air was not crowded with wings struggling to be the first out into the night.

Walter cracked an eye. Not a single memory flew through the window.

He turned the box around, looked inside.

Empty.

"There's been a robbery," Walter announced, his voice echoing through the otherwise vacant building. "Someone has taken Ruby's always stories! Someone has stolen the memories of Sullivan."

Geena
This Christmas

Something was off. I knew it the second I got home. Which is to say, back to Sullivan. Back to my girlhood house.

In the first place, Kurt, our mail carrier, had really crammed a bunch of items in my box—all kinds of junk mail, flyers and magazines and holiday ads. It stuck out at crazy angles, all smashed and wadded. It was completely unlike the neat rubber banded stack I was accustomed to.

I was tugging it out, trying to make sure I didn't miss anything important—not that catalogs addressed "To Resident" were ever that important—when Mrs. Cranston next door came outside to get in her car.

"Hey!" I called. "Mrs. Cranston! I was just about to go to the store myself."

Mrs. Cranston looked at me like I'd announced I was going to rush in my house to use the bathroom. Like somehow it didn't have anything to do with her—nor would she ever want it to.

I cleared my throat and adjusted my glasses. "I—thought maybe—we could go together. Buy ingredients for sugar cookies."

She stared blankly. I couldn't quite believe it. That whole summer after my parents' divorce, I'd gone running barefoot across the dewy morning grass that separated Dad's house from Mrs. Cranston's. We had baked together. A new recipe each day. Banana muffins and blueberry pancakes. Gooseberry pies and pineapple upside down cakes. It had been an escape from my bad feelings. From a half-empty house.

And after dad had died, Mrs. Cranston had shown up with the ingredients for gingerbread. We'd revived our baking routine. We'd even revived a bit of our dish-the-dirt, all that comfortable chatter that had once filled her kitchen. My father'd had a secret late-in-life girlfriend, she'd needed to confess as she added nutmeg—and quickly changed the subject.

But the way Mrs. Cranston was staring at me right then, it was like she didn't remember any of it.

"I thought—I could come over—we'd—drink some nog, whip up a batch of cookies?"

Some sort of recognition finally rippled across Mrs. Cranston's face. "Oh," she said. "Yeah." She stuck a finger through her white bangs to scratch her forehead. "I have so many errands. I need some yarn to finish a knitting project."

"When you get back, though—" I tried. But Mrs. Cranston had already turned away. She unlocked the door of her Civic and pulled out of her driveway.

Weird. It was definitely weird.

The weirdness only intensified when I tossed my bags

into the house and made my way to the square.

To begin with, the decorations were all wrong. For the past few years, the square had really been done up. City Council had hung vintage aluminum stars from the light poles. A tree had been brought in for the official Thanksgiving weekend lighting, decorated by art classes at the Sullivan elementary school. Front windows had been painted with candy canes. Wreaths hung from every shop door. Christmas music could be heard pouring out of cars. Sullivanites scurried about, plucking trees out of the nearby lot, shopping bags rustling as they bounced against their legs.

But this year, when I arrived, the stars weren't up. A semi-scraggly tree stood in the middle of the square, adorned with a sad looking string of tinsel and a sloppily crooked electric star as a topper, a giant cord hanging down to the ground with no attempt to conceal it in the branches.

A telephone line technician shimmied up a pole, whistling as he set to work. I shaded my eyes with my hand, catching a glimpse of the large red logo on the back of his coveralls. But his song sounded oddly out of tune.

Beneath him, one car blared its horn at another. "That was my space!" Pamela Krunk started screaming—so ferociously, the veins were sticking out from the sides of her neck.

"Aw, go get another," grumbled Susan Fitzweather, kicking her own door shut.

"You just wait till we get to the Senior Center," Pamela threatened vaguely.

It all felt so strange. A few years back, Sullivan had gone through a kind of downturn. Some had joked in the years before Angela's arrival that traffic had slowed to the point no one even thought it was necessary to repaint the faded lines of parking spaces. But Angela's reopening of Ruby's Place had definitely brought a kind of second wind to the square—more cars, more shoppers, more business openings. There had been such pride in the revival. And such desire to keep it going, let the little taste of success snowball.

Right then, though, if I'd had to pick a word to describe the way Christmas in Sullivan felt, I would have said *broken*.

The word rattled through me painfully.

Ruby's Place couldn't have been affected by this strange development, though.

Could it?

I got out of my car, the wind attacking my knee. I couldn't help it; I still loved ripped jeans. Child of the '80s and all. I hugged my gray wool coat—the vintage man's Pendleton jacket I'd been wearing for years—around my middle. And the first place I walked to was the old sidewalk square. The one with my name.

I felt a little predictable right then. Creature of habit.

The square, though, was anything but predictable.

The inscription that had withstood years of cold and hot temperatures, ice coatings and skateboards and delivery dollies, was crumbling. A chunk of *4Ever* was missing—a big enough chunk that it wasn't even legible anymore.

My first instinct was to burst inside and demand Angela tell me if she knew what had happened to it. Somehow, it felt like something important to me—something I had wanted to protect and keep safe—had been treated disrespectfully by the rest of Sullivan.

But I stopped when I saw Angela through the window—behind the bar, wiping a glass down. I must've seen her do that a hundred times. Always before, she delighted in it. Right then, she looked more like somebody who was daydreaming about escaping a job she hated, work that weighed on her.

An awful scraping sound traveled the length of my spine. I glanced up to see a little girl in a long braid dragging a stick against the brick walls.

"Maddie!" I called out.

She stopped walking. Turned to stare at me. Her arm stayed raised, her stick mid-scrape.

"It's Geena. Geena Barister. I was at Ruby's last Christmas. Remember? You played a song for your mom before we officially opened. Your song to her was her present. I still think about that."

"What for?"

"Because I—it was so sweet and—are you going to play Ruby's again this year?"

"Nah," Maddie groaned and started walking again, dragging her stick down the brick walls.

Confused, I wrapped my hand around the nail I still wore on a chain, every day, like a pendant necklace. I backed up, headed toward the trunk of my car. My hands were shaking a little as I hoisted out a cardboard box of books and carried it across the street, into The Page Turner.

"Hey there, hey there!" I called out, trying a little too

hard to sound festive and bright.

Kelly, Rob's lone employee, stopped shelving new arrivals. She glanced down at me—instead of waving, she offered what looked more like a shrug. And then she simply turned back to her job at hand.

"Hey, babe," Rob muttered. I tried to hang on tight to that *babe*. But something about his voice felt detached.

I waddled up toward the cash register, dropping my box on the counter top.

"You bringing in something for store credit?" Scott Drummond grinned at me. Was it warmly? I tried to believe so. It had to be. Didn't it? He'd just joked with me, after all.

I smiled and half-chuckled back. "I found these in Dad's bookcases," I admitted.

"Wouldn't happen to be a giant pile of Westerns, now would it?" Rob asked.

It would. As a matter of fact. The same Westerns Rob had once kept for Dad under the checkout counter. He'd made it a point to scour online auctions and estate sales for the rarest finds in Dad's favorite genre. When Dad showed up—as he did multiple times a week, forever on the lookout for a great read—Rob offered him a new box to dig through.

It was common for Rob to offer up such kindnesses; he regularly donated books to schools or veterans' facilities. He frequently added an additional free read to customers' bags—just because—when they stopped in to buy their paperbacks. He paid Kelly better than just about anybody in town. If someone hadn't known Rob's history, they probably would have assumed the Westerns were simply another thoughtful gesture. But Dad was more than just a customer. They'd shared something special, years ago.

They'd shared me.

I sometimes wondered what it had been like during all those face-to-face visits, Dad and Rob separated by the front counter at The Page Turner. I figured Rob had never mentioned ringing our doorbell week after week through high school, or calling the house looking for me, or eating dinners in the kitchen. I figured Rob never acted as though he'd once known every creaky step in our house. Or memorized the pattern of the living room wallpaper.

Dad certainly didn't have to buy his books there, either. But for some reason, when Rob had returned to Sullivan and bought the same bookstore the two of us had loved as kids, Dad had started showing up.

Maybe we all kind of keep getting drawn to old sore spots—the ache of wanting a father's approval, or the fear of perhaps being a father who might have overreacted to the possibility of his teenage daughter making a life-altering mistake. Like maybe we could somehow find the perfect salve. Finally find a way to soothe it.

And maybe, too, sore spots are really nothing more than stories that just aren't finished yet. Maybe we're all aching to find our own happy endings.

"Donation," I said, pushing the box a little closer to Rob. "Still cleaning out Dad's stuff." And grinned, like I was handing over diamonds. Stories, I'd often thought, were the most precious items in the world.

Rob had to agree. Here he was, in charge of so many

stories himself. Shelves and shelves of them. Pressed between covers branded with the storyteller's name. Stories depended on him.

And here I was trying to find a way to help. Since the store was struggling. Only so much struggling a business could do before it failed completely.

"Good for you, cleaning out the house," Scott said. "Clutter'll kill you."

I flinched. These books were special. Not trash. "Dad would've wanted these to come back to you," I said. And then promptly felt utterly ridiculous. Why would these old books help Rob's bottom line at all? Any more than any other book that walked through the shop's door?

"I found them in the closet. When I was getting out the Christmas lights," I explained, pretty lamely. Two minutes after I showed up in town, I was looking for external lights? Why was I still pushing these books toward Rob? Why was I so insistent? Wasn't I showing Rob that I knew he was in financial trouble?

"Does anybody actually like outdoor lights anymore?" Scott murmured.

"Maybe Angela's sister would," Rob suggested.

Scott and I both flinched that time.

"What?" Rob pressed.

"Where'd you get that idea?" Scott asked.

"From Angela," Rob said. "She and her sister get together every Christmas. She told me that. Said the two of them were planning their annual get-together the year she literally bumped into the old place. Ruby's, that is."

"But she—" Scott shook his head. "Guess you and Geena were kind of far behind me and Angela in school."

"What's that got to do—?" Rob started.

But Scott cut him off with, "Never mind. Think my own family's gonna skip the whole Ruby's Place thing completely this year."

"You are?" I asked, dumbfounded. Why wasn't he feeling a tug to return, to share another night there with his kids?

"Listen," he told Rob, "let me know what you find out about maybe getting me that signed edition, all right? Sure would help me out if I could get that Christmas gift for the wife lined up." He turned toward me. "Christmas shopping," he grumbled. "Such a pain."

Pain?

"Yeah," Rob muttered. "Sure."

As Scott left, Rob tugged my box the rest of the way off the counter, placing the lot of books by his chair, to be entered into inventory.

"Roads okay?" he asked. "Been pretty icy lately."

That was it? A question about the roads? No scooping me up, no hug that could crush my ribs, no hello kiss? No tucking my hair behind my ear, a sweet gesture that had always been the way he'd shown his affection—even when we were kids, before we'd shared our first kiss? Not even *that*?

I might have thought maybe something was up between us—that a rough patch was forming—had I not just seen so many other oddball happenings. Winter had settled in, and not just to make the outdoor skies gray and snowy. Winter had somehow invaded everybody's hearts.

The Gift That Is Ruby's Place

Something had happened to Sullivan.

Geena

As the days passed, the strangeness held on tight, like some sort of parasite had burrowed its head into the town and was sucking the lifeblood out of it.

Cyndi at the gas station on the highway put out the saddest excuse for fruitcake ever seen. Burned, crooked, and lumpy, the plastic wrap only partially covered the little loaves that had been tossed onto a table in a sort of *oh, who really cares, anyway?* sort of manner. The local radio station wasn't playing carols. Tina at the It Ain't Over Yet flea market was not decked out in a vintage Christmas sweater and green go-go boots—just a plain old black turtleneck. Sure, it was paired with '80s high-waisted jeans and fingerless gloves, vintage just like always. But it wasn't her usual red and green seasonal fare.

And I did not get the usual postcard invitation in the mail, the ones that Angela sent out in December, reminding everyone to come to Ruby's Place for marshmallows and cocoa and the warmth of the holidays.

I helped out at The Page Turner, showing up to cover the lunch rush that never seemed to be much of a rush. I was determined not to bring up the lack of shoppers, convinced it was a problem specific only to Rob's shop—until I happened to glance through the front window only to watch the wind catch the small wreath I'd tried to attach to the door and toss it across the empty square like a tumbleweed.

That was when it started to sink in: No "Sale" signs, not a single holiday front window display, and no foot traffic to be seen. Just that phone technician in his work coveralls, this time shimmying up a telephone pole near the bank. The square was more than just undecorated. In fact, the square resembled a shopping center *after* the post-Christmas get-rid-of-everything-left discounts.

"Where's everyone shopping this year?" I asked.

"Dunno," Rob admitted. "Don't hear much about gifts. Scott was one of the few coming in looking for a signed or deluxe edition of something. Mostly, it's just my regular customers. But then, that's dropped off a little, too. As I'm sure you've noticed."

I frowned. "Don't you find that strange?"

"Why? Gifts aren't everything."

"But how are people celebrating? Is Angela still holding her big Christmas Eve party? I never did get one of her postcards. I was hoping she just assumed we were on board with helping her out again."

"Oh, yeah," Rob muttered, as though the thought had just occurred to him. "I guess she usually does send reminders. You really want to go?" He made a face, scrunching up his mouth.

All I could think of, at that moment, was a Christmas Eve of my youth. And the silhouettes I had seen in the window when I'd glanced behind my shoulder, making sure no one suspected I'd just sneaked out. It was 1989—easy to remember the year, because Rob and I graduated the next spring. Rob had shown up to smuggle me out the kitchen door, leaving Mom to watch *It's a Wonderful Life* with my step-dad. We'd run—not down the street, but cutting through backyards, climbing over fences, to get to his giant Caprice parked on another block, out of the step-dad's watchful eye. My ankles burned by the time we crawled into the front seat, all that snow still packed onto my jeans. But it didn't matter.

It was hand-in-hand back then, and laughter—always laughter—and constant brainstorming about how to squeeze out a few more minutes together. Fifteen minute slices were never enough, but were never shrugged away, either. And in that Caprice, Rob had cranked the heat, turned on the radio, and taken me into his arms. Our embraces were not simple hugs, but struggles to get ever closer to one another, to show—a little bit better than we had the day before—just how strong our love was. He'd given me the nail on the chain that night, although that year, Rob had already given me about fifty little trinkets.

He'd given me his love, too—I'd felt that far more strongly than I'd ever felt wrapping paper under my fingernails. Oh, how we had loved, back then—do all young sweethearts feel this way?—with our whole hearts, unafraid of being hurt. In a way that should have exhausted us but never did.

"You don't—you don't want to go?" I asked. I wasn't sure what else to say.

"Eh, I dunno. It's always the same."

"Always the—" My voice tapered off. Didn't he re-member? Didn't he think of it—the way we'd laughed, run-ning through those backyards? How sweet those slices of time together were? I didn't live in Sullivan year-round anymore. These moments together on my university breaks should have been every bit as precious.

And yet, right then, Rob felt like a bad connection on the phone. The sort engulfed by static so loud the two of you just kept shouting and still never really heard one another. I found myself wishing I could call out to the technician out-side, get him to check the line between us, shore it up, make everything clear again.

Where are you? I thought, staring at him. The blow was bad enough that I retreated into the back of the store, fighting to make sense of it all and catch my breath.

Later that night, when I returned home, there it was. In the living room. Looming. Dad's old writing desk. I swear, the thing was actually growing. Getting taller. Calling out to me.

The bottom drawer might as well have had a spotlight pointed on it.

Ever since I'd come home, I'd cleaned around it. Tried to ignore it. As I stared at it, part of me wanted to throw that drawer open, give my chapters another look. But I was afraid. What if it was terrible? Or what if—and this would be far, far worse—what if it was good? And what if, reading it, I still had no idea where to go? How to finish it? What the ending should be?

It was torture.

In the end, I took the coward's way out. Turned the lights out. Headed to bed.

The next day, I started decorating the house. Hauled out the holly, as the song said. Tinsel and stockings and a tree from the attic. Somehow, it didn't look festive at all—only plastic.

Maybe, I thought, I needed something alive. Something real. So I headed to The Red Apple, the supermarket with the florist just inside the door. I picked up a poinsettia and carried it to the checkout counter, where Kimberly Tan was clipping dead pieces off table-sized pine trees.

"Hey, Kim," I said, trying on a cheerful tone. It was hard to get it to sound right, though, like a musical note out of my range.

She grunted back.

"Your kids must be excited about Santa coming," I tried. It had never been this hard to talk to Kimberly before. I had babysat her, lugging along books to study from or read once she had gone to sleep. In order to tire her out, we had often played gossip, in the same way other little girls played house. It involved sitting among all her stuffed animals and letting her teddy bear whisper into the ear of her stuffed pig, something she knew for a *fact* had happened to the long-eared plush rabbit. And, inevitably, dissolving into giggles. After Dad had died, she'd done a bit of whispering into the ears of other classmates—all of them showing up at Ruby's Place that Christmas Eve with their hugs and their smiles, making my holiday feel far less dark. Kimberly herself had put her hand on my arm, telling me that no snow was accumulating on the sidewalk square with my name and Rob's. ("Almost like *Rob & Geena 4Ever* is so hot, snow melts as soon as it hits," she'd said, teasing me playfully.)

Now, though, Kim stared me down harshly. "Kids don't believe in Santa anymore," she grumbled.

"Really? They're still kind of young to have abandoned all that, aren't they?"

Kim rang up my plant and returned to pruning the small trees. With the latest snip, I gasped, reached out to grab her wrist.

"What's with you?" she barked, glaring at me.

"You're—trimming green limbs," I told her.

Kim glanced at the tree again. She had cut nearly every single limb from the slender trunk in the center. Only two scraggly little arms remained, almost like that poor tree was reaching out, begging for help. Begging to be saved.

Kim shrugged and clipped one of the last two arms. Hooked a miniature candy cane around the remaining limb, and smacked the pot with a pricing gun. The snipped limbs remained like a prickly green blanket on top of the soil.

"Merry—Christmas," I tried, but Kim didn't respond.

"And to you, Geena," I muttered for her, under my breath, as I headed back out to my car.

I placed my poinsettia on my kitchen table, but it seemed as festive as an empty tree stand. I wasn't surprised when I checked the soil. It felt overly dry, like Kim hadn't been watering it.

Frankly, it was as if all of Sullivan was in the midst of

a holiday drought.

Angry and frustrated, I found myself pacing yet again in front of Dad's old writing desk. Muttering obscenities at it. "I can't avoid you forever," I grumbled, unlocking the bottom drawer.

I removed the manuscript and thumbed through the pages. But the words left me hollow. I remembered the way I'd felt writing them—like my dream was right there, inside my fingers.

Now, that dream felt like a love I'd once had and then lost.

I tossed the pages onto the coffee table, almost like a wrestler tossing an opponent to the mat.

"I lost you somewhere," I muttered to the book. My eyes narrowed. "I'm no stranger to that, though. Am I? Wasn't Rob also literally a love I once lost, then got back again?"

Maybe. The way he'd been acting since I'd come home, he sometimes seemed like I'd lost him a second time. Lost him with the rest of my hometown.

I guess a weaker woman would have crumpled onto the carpet, tears streaming. Or better yet, just gotten up the guts to finally trash the pages.

Me? I couldn't give it up. I paced, running my hands through my hair. "Idea, idea," I muttered, like repeating the word could somehow tug it out of hiding.

But I knew where my original idea had come from. It couldn't be that hard to tap into it, could it? I threw open the bottom drawer, snatching out the bottle I'd found in a snow pile last Christmas.

"*You* had an idea once," I told that bottle. "I tried you last year, after I wrote the first eight chapters. And you didn't work. At least, not for me. But maybe you'd give somebody else an idea. One that might help."

I grabbed my coat, tossed that bottle into the passenger seat, and backed out the driveway.

I drove, everything in my path gray and cold and winter-sad.

At the town square, I pulled myself from the car and dropped the old bottle into the deep side pocket in my Pendleton coat.

I started for The Page Turner, my original destination, but Rob was busy with someone at the counter—I could see them through the window—so I took a small detour, winding up at the history museum. It was late in the afternoon, but right then, I figured I could use a little feel-good infusion from the past.

I grabbed the door handle and tugged.

And nearly fell when the door wouldn't open.

I tugged again. The door refused. But the usual closing time painted on the entrance was not for another hour.

I knocked. "Toby?" I shouted, using the museum director's name. "Hello? Door's stuck."

A voice coming from behind me announced, "No, it's locked." Ms. Bryant, who'd coached thousands of Sullivan high schoolers through reading *The Iliad* in Latin, stood on the sidewalk, her hands stuffed deep in her pockets.

"Hey, there," I sighed, relieved to see her. "Coming to work? Got some sort of new holiday exhibit Toby put you in charge of? I'd love to see it."

She shook her head, but I kept on talking. "I mean," I went on, "Toby put you in charge of last year's, right? The Secrets of Sullivan. You've been working on getting an exhibit about Ruby's together for quite some time. Almost a year. Haven't you?"

But she was still shaking her head. "It's closed."

"For the night?"

"Indefinitely."

"The *history museum*?" I screeched that last part. "For what reason?"

"Lack of interest."

"Lack of—" I put my hand on my chest, like I was checking to make sure my heart was still beating.

But now that neither of us was talking, I could finally hear it: the silence.

And now that I'd noticed it, I had to admit to myself that it had been eerily quiet ever since I'd crossed the city limits. Not a single whisper coming from The Red Apple. Or from Kurt when he delivered the mail. Or from Rob, for that matter. Sullivan was a lot of things—but one thing it had never been was quiet. It had never minded its own business. It had never, not once, ever turned down a juicy tidbit.

"How can that be?" I squeaked. "We love our stories. Our gossip! Why would no one be interested any longer in the stories kept in the museum? Those are *our* stories. Right?"

I'd never seen Ms. Bryant look at me in that way. Back when I was eighteen, in her class, wearing my acid washed Palmetto jeans and my nail necklace, Ms. Bryant had looked at me with hope and encouragement. She'd be leaning close, kind of waving me forward with her hands. *You can get this*, she'd be saying with her eyes.

And that was how it always was in Sullivan. In this small town, where we were always watching and listening and whispering, didn't we all care? Wasn't that what had fueled the gossip? Not the desire to tear someone down, but to find out where we could help? Didn't the town show up for me a couple of years ago when Kimberly Tan had helped spread the news that Dad had died? Didn't we all want the best for each other?

And now?

"Gossip," I repeated. "If light bulbs could run on rumors, Sullivan wouldn't go dark..."

"I put up mini-exhibits," Ms. Bryant interrupted. "All year long. I was going to do an exhibit just on Ruby's, that's true. But I could never get it right. There's so much about it—an entire cabinet of donations in Toby's archives. Did you know that?"

I shook my head. I didn't know about the cabinet. But I did know exactly how sprawling Ruby's story was. I'd seen it for myself. My hand found the lip of the bottle in my pocket.

"So, while I was trying to figure it out, untangle everything, I put up little exhibits," Ms. Bryant explained. "Did one of the phone company. Got Tina to loan me her switchboard."

"Her—"

"—switchboard. She bought one at some farm auction. Old Southwestern Telephone switchboard. Used to have to call the operator when you needed to get in touch with somebody, and the operator would connect you manually. Actually plug the line in. Can you imagine? Tina started out thinking she'd sell it, but then—she decided not to. Swore the thing still lit up, all on its own. Said when you put a headset on, you could hear voices stuck inside. I went over there—I don't know, Tina's always saying stuff like that, how old items have stories locked inside—and I swear, I could hear it. Each different slot I plugged into let me hear the soundtrack of a different decade. Streets sound different depending on the era. Car engines sputter along differently. Voices are different. Kids play different games on the square. By the time you were a teenager, they were showing up with boomboxes, their music blaring. So I took the switchboard over on loan to the museum."

Linda fell quiet, her eyes going distant like she was remembering it all again.

"And—?" I asked.

"Turned out, nobody else could hear it. All those voices inside the switchboard. People on the tour would slip on the headset, plug the line in and—silence.

"Funny thing was, every single time somebody told me they couldn't hear anything, I'd try it myself, only to find the noises and the voices in the switchboard sounded a little farther away. Until..."

"Silence for you too."

"It was like everyone gave up after that," Linda said softly. "On the museum. Like not hearing discouraged everybody, almost."

Perplexed, I tightened my hold on the old bottle. "Last Christmas, you were at Ruby's, weren't you?" I asked. "I mean, you came in before the official opening."

"Yes, of course. You know that. You let me in early and handed me that drink. I felt a little strange about kind of barging my way in ahead of everyone else who was gathering on the sidewalk outside. I hadn't even planned to go that night. I felt like I got swept inside almost accidentally."

Why would she find it strange that she would have been ushered inside, out of the cold, on Christmas Eve? Weren't there always soft spots for old teachers? Didn't everyone see a teacher and remember, in a rush, how it felt to be seventeen? Wasn't the sight of an old teacher as powerful as seeing an old photo? Surely, Ms. Bryant had been waved to the front of hundreds of lines in Sullivan since her retirement.

"About that pre-opening toast. The drink I gave you," I started.

"Yes?" A flat point-blankness filled her answer.

"Did the cocktail," I pressed, "did it—make you see anything, or…"

"What, like stars?" Ms. Bryant asked. "Sure was some strong stuff. Never did experience anything quite like it."

"But did you see—"

"See what?"

Something about the way she said it made me feel a little shaky—unsure of what had even happened to me last Christmas. What had driven me to my keyboard. And I completely understood how Ms. Bryant could have wound up doubting she'd heard anything coming through the old switchboard.

"Well," she said. "I probably ought to get home." And without offering me so much as a *happy holidays*, she walked down the street.

"Ms. Bryant!" I called out.

When she turned, I pleaded, "Come back. Okay? Convince Toby to reopen. There's something—"

Something what? Everything was missing from Sullivan. Why would a bunch of old relics have any power to fix that?

Ms. Bryant drifted off yet again—disappearing around the corner—and I raced in the opposite direction, back toward The Page Turner.

As I grew closer to Rob's shop, my eyes roved upward the power lines. Black strings on a gray sky. Gray stone roofs nearby.

I stopped walking, swiveling to look up and down the street. Not a single red spot.

No cardinals. I couldn't recall seeing even one since I'd returned.

What was really wrong with Sullivan? Was a town more than just a place? Did a town have an actual heartbeat? Did that mean a town could die?

Frightened by my own thoughts, I burst into The Page Turner as Kelly started wrapping a scarf around her throat.

"See you tomorrow, Kel," Rob said.

"Uh-huh," Kelly muttered, stepping out into the glow of twilight.

Even the door didn't jingle happily to announce the

end of her workday. It just kind of clunked.

"Want me to flip it?" I asked Rob, my hand on the "Open / Closed" sign.

"Sure."

With the "Closed" portion turned toward the sidewalk, I edged my way closer to the counter. "You go through Dad's box?"

"Not yet."

He didn't even seem interested.

Heart hammering away, I leaned in, offered a, "Pssst."

Rob didn't turn.

"Psst."

Nothin'.

"*Psssssttttt!*"

Finally, he raised an eyebrow.

I tugged the bottle from my coat. "How 'bout a drink?"

I expected him to smile—or wink—or *something*, but he only snagged a couple of Styrofoam cups from the small table that held the coffee pot for customers. Free coffee to anyone who came by to browse.

"Want to know where this came from?" I asked, my hand on the bottle.

"Figured you found it in your house. Like maybe your dad had a hiding spot or something."

My heart thumped increasingly harder as he headed back toward the counter. I wanted this to help. After my interaction with Ms. Bryant, my faith was wavering. Faith in what, though—Sullivan? Gossip? Christmas?

All of the above, it seemed then.

I wanted him to take a sip. I wanted him to recognize the taste. I wanted him to have a flash, like I did on Christmas. I wanted him to say he had seen the past last Christmas too. I wanted him to tell me that magic was real, that he felt it, strong as ever.

I slid the bottle toward him. I was trembling, but I told myself this could do it. He would take a sip, and he would tell me he knew the truth about Ruby's Place. We could share that together. It could unite us, draw us closer.

And more. He would tell me what the liquor made him see this time, and I knew in my heart it would be the missing piece of my book.

But when Rob twisted the cap, he cringed. "Oh, Geena. That stuff's turned." He lunged out from behind the counter and reached for the shop's entrance.

"N—no," I tried, but before I could get to him, he was pouring the last of the bottle into the flowerpot just outside the shop. The one that usually held some sort of holiday plant. The one that was currently empty.

I felt as if he had poured out the last drop of magic in the world.

"What's that look for?" Rob snickered.

"I just—I—" I slipped the bottle from his hand. Stared at the withered piece of mistletoe still stuck inside.

"Why don't you go across the street?" Rob asked. "If you're in the mood for a cocktail, I bet Angela'd whip us up a couple of drinks. Be there in ten."

Standing there, staring at him, he felt like little more than an acquaintance. And the necklace I wore was indeed just some old worthless nail.

Geena

The problem of the book was one thing, but underneath that, I'd wanted to share something else with Rob. I'd wanted him to see—all in a single gulp of that liquor—not just the truth of Ruby's Place, but that two years ago, in that very bar, on Angela's first Christmas Eve serving up cocoa and holiday spirit, I saw my dad.

The whole night had been magical, really. Even before I'd seen Dad. Surely he remembered. From the moment we'd stepped inside, everyone at Ruby's had cheered for me and Rob—a real-life "Jack and Diane" love story, two Midwest kids, our tale made famous by a piece of graffiti that could never be scrubbed away. Love, they'd felt certain when they looked at us—back together again, our fingers all intertwined in one another's—was not fragile or flimsy. It remained. It was an ornament you could wrap up in tissue, store away in an attic, and know it would always be where you left it, waiting for you to return.

We'd believed that, too, sneaking off for stolen moments in the back room of Ruby's. There was something so special about the feel of the night—the past was with us, making sure that the time apart didn't matter nearly as much as the time we'd once had together. 1989 was right there with me—the front seat of Rob's car and the radio blaring hair metal songs of lost love, and me swearing to Rob, "That'll never be us." That certainty, the feeling of love being set in stone, love being something you could not change your mind about, was back.

As Rob was back.

That night of the reopening, in the midst of the crowd and the carols, the songs and the tears and the hugs, in the midst all the lovely, elegant times that were still right there, right where *everybody* had left them—there he was.

Dad. After his heart attack. After the celebration of his life. There he was, at a table for two, holding a seat for me. Looking younger than he had in ages. Smiling at me. Waiting for me.

What can I say that was like? A second chance and a renewal, wrapped in shock and tied with a ribbon of bliss.

I rushed to him. He rose to meet me. His hug felt exactly like my heart remembered.

He did not feel like a ghost. He felt real. I held his hand.

"I found your note," I told him. "First love. That was what you wrote." It had been such a strange turn of events: Dad sending me to The Page Turner, Dad writing me a note, Dad passing away all in what felt like a single breath—his last. "Needed a new read. Yeah, right," I muttered, staring into Dad's wide eyes. "A new Western," I scolded in a teasing tone, not angry at all. "Like you didn't have a hundred at the house already. A Western that you wouldn't let me download or grab from a bargain shelf at Walmart. Had to be The Page Turner, you said. Great Western shelf, you insisted. Get real. You wanted me to go out there. To see Rob. Didn't you?"

He'd smiled at me, his mustache kind of curling up and around. I'd pleased him. I was sure of it.

"Well, we're here. Together. Me and Rob," I'd said, tears streaming as I tried to point him out.

"Oh, hon, I wasn't trying to tell you what to do," Dad had said, with tears in his own eyes. "Whatever happens next...I'll be glad, Geena, whatever it is, if it makes you happy. But I don't want you to feel like it has to be Rob because I sent you out there. Don't think I was trying to tell you who to love. Who to marry. If to marry. Hopefully, you'll one day recapture the euphoria of a first love. But you don't need me to make good life choices. You can do that fine on your own."

I was still sure he must have wanted it. I wanted it, too. Wanted Rob for me, I mean. But I also wanted to show Dad how much his opinion meant to me. I wanted him to know I was listening.

"I'm so glad to know you're here," I blubbered. "To know I can still come see you."

"No," Dad said, quickly and somewhat harshly. "We won't see each other again. Not after tonight."

"Won't—why not? Why can't—"

"Listen. It's important you hear this. Rob grew into a really good man," Dad said. "I'll admit it. Better than I would have believed when you two were kids. And you've grown into a great woman. You were happy with him once. And I had you and Rob on my mind because—well." He paused, letting a smile etch itself into his cheek. "When I was about the age you are now, love came to me a second time."

That was when I saw her, stepping out of a shadow, it seemed. Heading straight for Dad. Pretty, shoulder-length blond hair. Red lipstick. A silky gray dress with long gauzy sleeves and a pleated skirt. She was older, I thought—fifty-five at least.

Did I know her? Did she seem familiar? A dress shop. That was it. She had appeared in advertisements for her own store, an upscale destination from a bygone era that still drew crowds, and remained, in my own youth, the store where mothers took daughters to buy special occasion dresses: holidays and proms and school orchestra performances and honor roll inductions.

As she continued to walk closer, Dad went on, "The woman I met, she was older than me, even. It happens, Geena. It does. If you're open to it. I was a little afraid you'd started to think you'd outgrown it. I thought maybe, by seeing Rob again, you would remember how great real love can feel. I thought it'd open you up to the possibility. Love isn't only for the young."

The woman tried to place a hand on his shoulder. But she thought better of it, took a step backward.

"Hello, Elizabeth," he'd said softly. He'd taken her hand. Held her in an embrace. And they had danced into a shadow.

I could hardly believe it. This was the late-in-life secret

girlfriend Mrs. Cranston had spoken of? The big-time celebrity everyone had murmured Elizabeth had been with was... my dad?

It was almost too good to be true.

As the months passed, I grew increasingly certain of it: *too good to be true.* Talking to him had only happened in my imagination.

It's so painfully easy to dismiss wonderful things. *Ever notice that?* I wanted to ask Rob. The mysterious. The inexplicable. As Christmas Eve faded, and snow melted, and decorations came down, I found myself wondering—what had I really seen? A wish? Fueled by wine? By the need to know I wasn't doing something stupid with Rob? To make the ground feel a little less wobbly? To soothe the fresh wound Dad's death had slashed across my heart? Had I simply liked the idea of him being with the elegant woman who'd sold me my graduation dress? Being seen by the rest of Sullivan as a man dashing enough to be confused with a movie star?

And then—one year to the day after seeing Dad in Ruby's, on *last* Christmas Eve—I found the bottle. Out in the snow. When I drank from it, I saw the past. I saw the truth of Ruby's Place. And I knew that my time with Dad had been *real.* Not just wishful thinking. Not nostalgia. Not too good to be true. I had seen Dad. Telling me that love wasn't only for the young. Dreams came late in life—he'd been insistent on that, too.

Thanks to the bottle, I'd gotten not quite halfway through my book only to abandon my own dream. *That* would have disappointed Dad. I knew that. Because I had disappointed myself.

"You comin'?" Rob called, pulling me out of my reveries of the last couple of Christmas Eves. There I was, still outside The Page Turner, still with the bottle in my hand. As if it didn't really matter what I wanted, he passed me by, heading for Ruby's Place. No arm around my shoulder, no hand in mine, no kiss on my cheek. "You don't get a move on, I'll have to drink yours for you," he warned. No attempt to tug me close. No turning to wink over his shoulder.

I shoved the bottle into the deep side pocket of my coat. Even empty, I wasn't willing to let go of it yet.

Not-So-Happy Hour

"Everything is wrong," Walter grumbled later that night.

"What's that?" Angela asked, listlessly wiping the inside of a martini glass.

"Everything is wrong," he repeated, louder that time.

She frowned, clunked the glass back onto the rack.

All around them, the after-hours happy hour continued, but it didn't sound joyful. Not anymore.

The crowd had thinned noticeably. By then, only five faces remained. Five of the once impossible to count regulars. Across the room, Evie was seated by herself, lazily playing an improvised piano melody with one hand. The other four—Ruby, Tom Barister, Elizabeth, and Walter himself—remained clustered around the bar, near Angela.

"Surely you feel it," Walter told Tom, who sipped from a beer while spinning a coaster on the surface of the bar.

"Why me?" he asked.

"Your daughter—your own Geena—she was just here. With Rob. I saw them. I came to get *you* to see them. I know you didn't talk to her, you had to see her from a distance, but did she seem the same to you?"

Tom shook his head. "Oh, her Christmas doesn't have anything to do with me anymore." At his side, Elizabeth—his lady love—sat staring at the mirror behind the bar, looking like a student dazed with boredom, chin in her hand. Even though her Tom had appeared in the same police officer blues he'd been wearing the night they'd met. Not his preferred flannel shirt, the one he'd kept long after a hole had appeared in the right elbow. *A man in a uniform*, Elizabeth could always be counted on to sigh with admiration.

That night? Not so much as a second look.

"You talked to Geena!" Walter said, pointing at Angela. How could he be the only one who noticed she was not her usual cheery holiday self? How could they all not see the changes in themselves?

"What if I did talk to her?" Angela asked. "Nothing unusual about it."

"Nothing—" Walter couldn't believe what he was hearing. He placed his hands on the top of his head. "But *everything* is unusual. Don't you guys feel it? The whole bar. It's just different."

Still, no one could so much as muster up the energy to argue with him. Or attempt to find out what was really bothering him.

"Rubes," Walter said. "Aren't you making some old-time drinks this year? Isn't Frankie teaching you how to make some of those Prohibition cocktails?"

Ruby simply turned her attention back to the front window. "She hasn't been by lately," she admitted, but seemed uncharacteristically withdrawn.

"Hasn't—?" Walter asked, surprised. "When did she stop coming?"

"Magic," Angela grumbled. "Isn't that what everybody said last year? Didn't we all think that Frankie had left something magical behind, for Ruby to tap into all those years ago, when she first opened the place? Didn't we come to think the building itself was magical, that it contained some—I don't know—spirit of endurance, at the very least? But where is Frankie now? Where did she go? Some endurance."

"Don't you think we're going to have a huge gathering on Christmas Eve?" he asked Angela, trying to appear positive.

"Oh, I doubt it."

"You—why would you doubt it?" Walter demanded.

"Why would people come to a bar on Christmas, anyway?" Angela grumbled. "They have other things to do."

"Why—you of all people should know the answer to that better than anyone!" Walter bellowed.

Angela squinted at him. "You're just obsessing over the Memory Bank."

Walter frowned. "How is it that no one else is?" he asked.

"Oh, come on, Walter. We still remember each other," Angela answered simply, pointing toward Tom and Elizabeth. "If the Memory Bank going empty were truly a problem, wouldn't we all suddenly have amnesia? Wouldn't we be strangers to each other?"

Walter had no answer for that. "Where is your *hat?*" he

pressed, leaning closer to Angela.

"My hat?"

"The one your sister gave you."

"Home. Somewhere."

"How can you say that? Your hat? Your hat. You wear it every year. When Christmas starts to roll around again."

"It's so ugly. It always was. First attempt, you know."

"But made by your own sister's hands."

Angela gave him one of those *so what* looks. It made him shiver. Or maybe what he really did was more of a sputter—like a light threatening to go out.

***

Walter had to get out of the bar. He had to see Sullivan for himself—in the daylight. Find out just how far the changes had permeated. If Geena had changed, had the entirety of Sullivan soured, too? He was desperate. No one at Ruby's Place was taking him seriously.

He wasn't exactly sure what he would be risking. A few of the other spirits had been outside of Ruby's—but only when absolutely imperative. He had himself perfected the art of taking trips to the Bank of Sullivan after nightfall, when the square was empty and no one would see him. Once he was out there in the sunlight, outside of Ruby's, would he be invisible to the people of Sullivan? Would any of the current residents be able to recognize him? Perhaps, he thought, he should wear some sort of disguise, just to be safe. He was being irrational. He knew it. And yet, while Angela was waving at Kurt, talking him up for a moment as he pulled her daily mail from his bag, Walter slipped behind a door marked "Lost and Found."

Surely, he thought, some Sullivanite in for an evening drink would have left behind an overcoat he could wear. He could raise the collar—pull his hat down. Maybe add some sunglasses. Did sunglasses look out of place in the winter?

"Oh, sorry," he said, finding the space occupied. He'd been expecting a pile of stuff. Cardboard boxes. Maybe a table or two. Not a room crammed full of people.

He tried closing the door. But a rather large woman, in a skirt and somewhat orthopedic looking black heels, was holding it shut. She shook her head at him, sending her brown hair scattering along her jawline.

"Don't tug too hard on that thing, chum," she told him. "Got a bad back, you know."

"Who are—" he started, even though he felt he already knew.

"Frankie. Hall. Used to—"

"—own this building when it was a speakeasy," Walter finished. Here she was. Inside the bar all along. Why had Ruby not seen her? Was Frankie hiding?

"And that's Edna, my old bartender," Frankie went on. "And Rose, who used to work the switchboard for the phone company. Used to connect all my calls. And Dorothy and Chester over there were my entertainment." She pointed, and on cue, Edna, Rose, Dorothy, and Chester nodded their hellos. They looked as though they'd stepped from a movie set during the Great Depression, the women with their bobbed hair and red lips, Chester in a pair of wool pants and suspenders. "Never will find two people who can make better music than Dorothy and Chester," Frankie swore, nodding at the trumpet in Chester's lap. Dorothy scooted a bit closer to her husband, the light rippling across her ivory sateen performing gown.

"Sorry. I thought I had the lost and found," Walter muttered, attempting again to close the door. He had no idea what this group was up to. He only knew that he felt he'd interrupted something.

"Yeah, well, whaddaya lookin' for? What, exactly, do you think you've lost?" Frankie asked. She raised an eyebrow, waiting for an answer.

"Well, I didn't exactly lose it, but I was hoping for an overcoat of some sort. I thought—this…is *this* the lost and found?"

"Yes, it is," Frankie told him. "This old building has two now. One full of coats and umbrellas, wallets and gloves left behind by the current *living* customers. And another one for us." She made a circular motion with her arm to include all the others.

"What're—why would you be in a lost and found?" Walter asked.

"'Cause we're in limbo. Not completely forgotten, not quite remembered, either," Frankie said.

"Angela fixed that, though. Didn't she?" Walter asked. "When she reopened the place? How could this be happening?" When he got no answer, he tried, "How long have you all been here?"

"Different lengths of time," Frankie said. "I was one of the first. Every once in a while, a new face comes to join us. I've been in here since shortly after last Christmas."

Walter was still trying to take this in when a young woman stood, offering him a wool topcoat old-fashioned enough to have perhaps belonged to Chester. "Here," she said, draping the coat across his shoulders. Walter's head was spinning to the point that he couldn't figure out if he recognized the woman or not. Young. Red sweater. Dark hair. Had he met her before?

He started toward the door when a thought came to him. He turned, asked, "Why don't you just leave?"

Frankie pushed him aside, stuck her arm through the open doorway. Her hand instantly disappeared, all the way up to nearly her elbow. She cringed, tugged her hand back. She was still frowning as she rubbed her arm. "Such a strange tingling," she muttered.

"You really can't get out," Walter said.

"You got it. Not that any of us knows what we can do to change that," Frankie grumbled.

"Hang on," he told the faces in the room. "I'm going to figure this out."

Tina

Mostly, that year, Tina missed the compliments.

She hated to admit it. Even to herself. It made her sound vain. *Hollow as an old tin can*, as her father might have said.

But there it was: she missed the compliments.

She had always suspected the praise had come with a twinge of sarcasm. Disbelief, at times. A little chuckle. But her vintage ensembles—the platform shoes, the wigs, the bell bottoms, the poodle skirts, the gaudy costume jewelry suites—had always gotten her attention. Pumping gas, stopping at the grocery for milk. Even just heading to work. She'd been a regular walking billboard for the It Ain't Over Yet.

That year, though, the compliments had fallen away. Almost like petals from a dead daisy.

Tina sighed, staring out at her displays. She had strung tinsel on the shelves. She had put blinking multi-colored lights up, all around the edges of the switchboard in the back. The one she had loaned the history museum. The one that Linda had returned a week earlier than anticipated.

"Did you put a recording in it?" Linda'd asked. "Some tape or something?"

Tina'd shaken her head.

"The voices inside are gone," Linda'd told her. "Figured something inside it had broken. Or gotten disconnected."

But Tina hadn't done anything to the switchboard. Not really knowing what Linda was talking about, she slammed the headphones on and listened, plugging the lines into one spot after another.

Linda was right. The voices had disappeared.

Doubt infected her. She began to wonder if the voices had never been there to begin with. Did Christmas turn people gullible? Make them dream up silly childish things?

Voices in the switchboard, Tina scolded herself. *Really.*

Tina'd put those mid-century plastic rosy-cheeked Santa faces—the ones that almost had a Kewpie doll look about them—all over the front window.

But they hadn't drawn in the shoppers. Not like they usually did.

She had even put a special arrangement together in the glass case that supported her cash register. A kind of Great Depression collage. Such a strange thing to gravitate toward during the holiday season. And yet, it had consumed her. She'd filled the case with tin toys and buffalo nickels and Nancy Drew books. Eisenberg pins and 1933 World's Fair memorabilia. Celluloid hair combs and a fragile paper diner menu. A cloche hat, one that looked awfully familiar. Just like the picture of the old-time singer behind the bar in Ruby's. Not that she could quite remember where she'd picked it up.

Beside her register, she'd placed a Bakelite radio, and tuned it to a local jazz station.

Most of the time, she didn't recognize the song playing. She'd never followed jazz. But every once in a while, she'd catch an instrumental version of "Sentimental Journey." And it would do something to her—mostly, for some reason, it was the sound of the trumpet that snagged her attention.

It tickled some part of her heart. She thought, distantly, that something had happened the year before. Something about a trumpet that had been brought to her store. It had been beautiful, she remembered. White metal. Carved all over with flowers and vines.

A man had come for it. Wasn't that right? A man who needed that trumpet? Because it would help him win back his lady love?

Tina shook her head at herself. "What a silly story," she grumbled. Had she read that somewhere? One of the paperbacks she'd picked up from The Page Turner? Some shred of gossip overheard at the Curly Girl Beauty Emporium?

Like all things sweet and kind that season, it felt made up. And objects didn't feel powerful at all. They didn't feel to her like they contained history or time or sweet sentimentality. Mostly, it all just felt like a bunch of junk.

Walter's Spy Work

He wandered the square, lingering at corners. He leaned on streetlights. He meandered into the diner. He walked the aisles of The Page Turner.

Walter still didn't understand what was happening. The people of Sullivan nodded hello to one another. They spoke. They called each other by name.

Angela was right—the residents of Sullivan had not forgotten each other. They recognized each other.

But something wasn't right.

Circling back, Walter encountered two men coming face to face on the sidewalk outside of Ruby's. Timothy and Glenn. Lifelong Sullivanites. Shaking hands. Trading bits of small talk. Offering a few vague promises, something about an exchange of gifts, though clearly neither had bought something for the other. In fact, neither could quite even put so much as a finger on what the other enjoyed. Was it fishing? Camping? Did Glenn have a daughter? What was Timothy's wife's name again?

To Walter, their conversation sounded brittle. It crackled like limbs in an ice storm. And it reeked with insincerity. These were offerings not meant to last. Empty promises used as polite excuses to move on, get away from one another.

A similar scene had played out once before, Walter remembered. The same night that Angela had made her overdue return to town. That year, these same two men had stood in front of the then-defunct Ruby's Place—a building growing ever more derelict with time—and had promised to get their families together. Walter remembered how hollow their words had sounded then. It had shattered his heart to think that promises had become disposable. Used once, tossed to the side, never any intent to make good on them.

It had also made getting Angela on board with reopening Ruby's all the more important. He'd known that as soon as her face had appeared on the opposite side of the plate glass, looking inside.

Walter frowned watching the two men part ways.

But just as Glenn was about to make his getaway, he pointed toward Ruby's Place. "Wife and I went last year," he mumbled.

"Yeah?" Timothy asked.

Glenn made a grunt that mostly sounded like an agreement. "My wife and I had our first date here."

Walter felt a cold wind blow straight through him. There it was again: three years ago, Glenn had told Timothy about this very first date in a wistful manner. A slight smile had revealed the sweetness and the specialness of it all, how he had prized his ability to tap back into the memory of that first night spent with the woman who would be his bride.

This time, though, Glenn was looking into the bar with a blank expression. The business was open; the opportunity to walk back inside was waiting on him.

And yet...

"Doubt we'll go again this year," Glenn admitted, in a disengaged sort of manner.

"Mom had a friend who used to play piano in there," Timothy murmured.

"Yeah?" Glenn grunted.

"Yeah."

Walter waited, hopefully, but the story stopped there. No reminiscing by Timothy about how Evie had looked in her special sequin jacket, the way she had always smelled of rosewater. Or how Timothy had once spent a Christmas Eve sitting beside her on the piano bench playing "Chopsticks" and "Heart and Soul" and the repeating chords in "Jingle Bells." Or that she had even let Timothy keep her tips that night—and how her gesture had stayed with him. How it warmed him inside anytime he thought back on it.

They both fell quiet again, staring at the entrance of Ruby's Place. Neither of them seeing farther than the green door. The bright sharpness of their memories had dulled.

They nodded goodbyes, signaling the moment had passed.

Not that it was really much of a moment to begin with.

They simply returned to the bustle of their current lives, to scraping snow from car windows and getting home before the meatloaf dried out.

Walter scrambled into the bar. "Angela!" he shouted.

"Angela!"

She emerged from the kitchen, a confused frown on her face. He was not where he was supposed to be. In a coat that didn't belong to him.

He batted away her questions. It didn't matter that he had been out on the street during the day. She had to look past that. He had the answers to what had happened to the spirit of Sullivan. He *knew*.

"I need to talk to you about what's going on in town. I've figured it out! It *is* the missing deposits from the Memory Bank," Walter insisted. "You're right, we haven't forgotten each other. We know names and faces. Now, anyway. We know what we've done together. But we don't remember our feelings. Who we are to each other. We don't remember the places we have always occupied in each other's hearts. *That's* what was in the Memory Bank. That's what we've lost."

The look on Angela's face remained blank. Unemotional.

"Don't you see? Once we've forgotten what we mean to each other, then the rest begins to follow. We're forgetting who people are—what they love, what makes them tick. Soon, it will be names and faces and events. Once the feeling is gone, everything else goes, too."

Walter's mind raced about desperately, as he tried to figure out a way to reach her.

"Where did you say your hat was?" he asked.

"Oh, Walter, quit harping on that hat. It's such an awful thing. I should throw it away."

Walter staggered back a step in shock. "Aren't you

looking forward to seeing your sister?"

Angela sighed. "My sister died when I was a kid. You know that."

"But you—"

"—had hoped to see some sort of vision of her?" Angela shook her head at herself. "Such silly dreams I had. Probably fueled by not feeling as though I measured up one Christmas. I guess maybe it was even kind of selfish. Hoping some vision would show up and instantly make me feel better about myself."

"It was your dream, though."

"We let silly things go when we grow up," Angela conceded. "I don't know what took me so long."

***

Walter lurched back into the lost and found. He weaved through the room, stopping in front of the girl in the red sweater.

"May I ask your name?"

"Gail."

"Gail Lowe?"

"Yes."

"Angela's sister?"

"Yes."

Walter squinted at her. "She waited for you. Christmas Eve for the last two years. She went to that back table. She wanted you to come. Where were you?"

Gail stood and made a motion for Frankie to move to

the side. When she did, she exposed a man seated on a bench at the back of the room, holding his head in his hands. His whiskers were scraggly, his grease-stained overalls worn thin. He removed his large felt hat, squeezing it flat beneath his blackened fingernails.

"Everybody drank from the bottle," he said. Or maybe that was croaked. His voice was gruff. Raspy. Almost a growl.

"What bottle?" Walter asked.

"Maxwell's Special Blend."

"Maxwell—Ross?" The name had permeated the air in Sullivan throughout Walter's own boyhood. Maxwell's misfortunes were legendary. Dark clouds had not followed Maxwell so much as they had anticipated his every next step, ensuring they would already be overhead whenever Maxwell showed up.

Walter felt himself tightening up, getting ready for some sort of hardship or setback to vibrate throughout the lost and found at the mere appearance of Maxwell's name. And then—as was usual for Sullivan—the stories exploded.

"Maxwell and I had the same idea, back in the Depression." The man put his hat on the seat beside him. He stood, extending his hand for Walter to shake. "Robert Ludlow," he said. "Frankie's liquor supplier."

"Robert here was a mechanic by trade," Edna, Frankie's old bartender, agreed. "Used to do plenty of repair jobs for me and my husband."

"But there wasn't much work back then—nobody really had to have a car to get around Sullivan," Ludlow explained. "So I made me a still. Maxwell did the same over at

160

his family farm. But by the time he got his up and running—"

"Ludlow was already my sole liquor provider. We'd already struck a deal. And I'm a woman of my word," Frankie added proudly.

"And Maxwell was never a man who could ignore the desire for revenge," Walter finished.

"He called me," Rose chimed in. "The night of the bust at Frankie's. I was there working the switchboard. He had me connect to Ludlow. Told him Frankie needed a Christmas Eve delivery. Then Maxwell had me connect to the police station, where he reported an anonymous tip. Not that I knew back then that was what he was doing." Her face twisted up with the guilt she had surely always carried.

"Unlucky to begin with," Ruby added, walking into the lost and found, "Maxwell's life became a tragedy after that. No one wanted anything to do with him after it came out he'd taken Frankie down. With no one willing to give him honest work, desperation sent him from one less-than-legal scheme to another, with breaks coinciding with various jail sentences."

She eyed Walter in a way that said this was why she hadn't wanted to talk much about Frankie's absence before. A way that said she was well aware of the lost and found—had been for some time—but not relegated to it like the other faces.

Not yet, anyway.

"My opening year," Ruby added, "Maxwell was determined yet again to get revenge. Instead of seeing his life as something he had brought on himself, he just blamed everyone in Sullivan for his hard times. So in '55, he took some mistletoe off the wreath on my own front door. Dropped it in one of his last remaining whiskey bottles. Switched the labels so I'd think the bottle was full of my favorite rum."

"Mistletoe?" Walter asked.

"Mistletoe is poisonous," Dorothy told him.

"That bottle got pushed to storage," Ruby said. "Until last year."

"Last year?" Walter asked.

"The toast!" Frankie announced loudly. "Before opening night last year. Everybody took a sip. Of Maxwell's Special Blend."

She continued on, her face getting red and sweaty as her details piled up. But Frankie wasn't the only one who had something to add. They were all talking, every single one of them. Like the gossipers they'd always been.

But then a funny thing happened. The words all started to take on a strange kind of glow. *If light bulbs could run on rumors, Sullivan wouldn't go dark for a thousand years*, the old saying had always gone.

And at that moment, their stories combined to create a brilliant white flash—like the world's brightest light bulb. As the glare started to fade, the scenery all around Walter looked different. He was no longer in the lost and found, but in the center of Ruby's. Evie was pounding away on the piano, and Dorothy was signing. The place was utterly packed with the trappings of Christmas—mistletoe and pine and cocoa and marshmallows. Waves of laughter, and couples dancing and kissing, and shouts of, "Angela, you've outdone yourself!"

"Reminds me of the times when Ruby ran this place." "It's perfect, Ang! Your opening night's a success!"

Clearly this was Christmas Eve of two years ago—Angela's first as the new owner of Ruby's.

The night passed on fast forward. And at the end of it all, Angela crammed an ugly brown hat on her head, carried her cocoa to the table in the back, and she sat.

"Hey, kiddo," Gail said, appearing on the opposite side of the table.

Angela didn't answer. She drummed her fingers.

"Ang?" Gail asked, as Angela looked through the window, to the street outside. "Ang?"

But Angela continued to glance around. She bit her nails. She tried humming "It's Beginning to Look a Lot Like Christmas."

"Angela!" Gail waved her hands in front of her sister's face.

The cocoa cooled. Angela wiped the tears from her eyes. She stood, gathering the cups, and walked away.

When Angela turned off the Ruby's Place neon sign, Walter's vision of that Christmas Eve went with it.

Walter blinked himself fully into the present, staring at the expectant faces in the lost and found. All of them quiet, their stories having wound down.

For the moment, at least.

"You *were* there for Christmas," Walter told Gail.

"I've been with her every step of the way," Gail said softly. "Through renovations and money worries, all those struggles to get the place back up and running. I was there

163

right at the beginning, too. Who do you think pushed her into the door, the first year she came back to town? Pushed her hard enough—and wore a coat big enough—that she mistook me for a man, it seems."

"And now, after not seeing you for the last two Christmases—" Walter said.

"She's let me go," Gail finished. "Not just temporarily. Not this time. This isn't about a little girl growing up and finding her own way. She's given me up for good. Hasn't she?"

"No. Not completely. Not yet," Walter insisted. "You're still here, aren't you? In a place where you could still be claimed."

Gail shook her head, ready to dismiss him.

"It's the Memory Bank." Walter looked across the room, at the faces surrounding him. "The Memory Bank was robbed sometime after last Christmas," he told them all. "I couldn't release all those remembrances. The feelings associated with the times we hold dear. They couldn't fly out to tickle the minds of the people of Sullivan. Without being reminded, I'm afraid…I'm afraid…"

"You think it's all falling apart," Gail finished. "Memories aren't permanent. They can fade without safekeeping."

"And I didn't keep them safe," Walter lamented. "I thought the bank would be the right place." He rubbed his forehead.

"I don't buy that's it," Ludlow growled. "Not completely. Got to have something do to with Maxwell's bottle. I'm sure of it. The bottle got out last Christmas. After the toast. But I don't know where it went."

"It's my switchboard," Rose argued. "No one can see us, but no one can hear us, either. Our voices used to fill that old switchboard in the flea market. When I first came to town, I used to work it. Used to connect the past and the present. But no one could hear, and I wound up in this room..."

"It's all of it tied together," Gail said. "It has to be. Everything's so different. Even Angela. The past few Christmases, when she's tried to visit me, her heart hasn't been in the same place. She expects something external—this bar—to do the trick. But it can't. Her belief in the magical isn't the same. Not like it was when she was a kid..."

Walter shivered at the appearance of a new thought. "Where is Maxwell?" he asked.

Everyone only stared at him.

"Maxwell was quite the story," Frankie said, "back when we all lived and worked in Sullivan. But these days?" She scrunched her face and shook her head. "Not anymore. He's never been here in the lost and found."

"At least," Chester added, "not with us."

"Meaning?" Walter asked, but he sucked in a sharp breath when the answer came to him. "Meaning he may have been here before you. And when no one claimed him..."

"When the memories go, so do we go," Frankie said. "Soon, this room will be empty. The bar will be empty. Every spirit will gone. Oblivion. Just like Maxwell. Including you."

These faces had all had these fears before. They'd always run the risk of being forgotten. But never before had the possibility of it felt more real.

They were all in greater danger than they'd ever been.

Of that, Walter was certain.

Walter's Search

Walter didn't have to wait long for the after-hours happy hour to wind down that night.

Like the previous nights, it wasn't much of a happy hour at all. But even more so that night, it seemed.

When Ruby's Place cleaned out of the small number of remaining regulars, he raced toward Angela's bottles. Top shelf, storage, back room. He had lost track of how long he'd been at it when he felt someone standing at his side.

"What is all this?" Tom asked, pointing at the bottles spread out on the floor, stacked on the tables, and lined down the length of the bar.

Walter sighed with relief. "I should have called you sooner," he confessed. "Everything keeps disappearing. The memories. The voices in the switchboard. And now, it seems, a bottle."

"Bottle?" Tom repeated. "Looks like missing one couldn't do you much harm."

Walter glanced all around, at the sea of glass glimmering in the overhead lights.

"Nobody's called me in an official capacity before. Not since I became an after-hours regular at Ruby's, anyway," Tom acknowledged, hooking his thumbs into the belt on his police uniform, the same he'd worn throughout his daughter's youth. The same he'd hoped would put a little healthy intimidation into Rob. (What father wasn't ever at least a little suspicious of his daughter's first love?) The same uniform he generally only wore these days to please or impress Elizabeth. "Not quite sure how I'd put out an APB on missing whiskey."

"You were the only person I could think of. I have to find it. You have to help me," Walter said. His jacket was off, tossed into a crumpled wad in the middle of the floor. Shirtsleeves rolled. Tie loosened.

"Find what? Some bottle?"

"An antique bottle that belonged to Maxwell Ross. He—well. The story's long, and the details don't matter right now." They did, though. They mattered more than almost anything Walter could think of. It was only that he couldn't explain it, not how Maxwell fit into all of it, exactly. Or how it could be possible that he was still wreaking havoc even though he was no longer anywhere close to Sullivan. Walter only felt certain it was part of the bigger puzzle, part of what was wrong, something that was maybe doing damage to Sullivan and had to be tracked down. "What's important," he wound up saying, "is that what's inside has been poisoned. With mistletoe. And the bottle—I think it might have gotten out."

"Wait," Tom said, a deep kind of concern flashing across his face. "A bottle? With mistletoe?"

"I just can't imagine what could have happened," Walter said, running his hands through his hair as he reexamined the labels on the bottles, wondering if he'd missed something. "I—"

But when he turned to face Tom again, he found Ruby's empty.

***

Tom raced straight back to his old house, the one where he and Geena had shared so many happy years. That night, though, the living room had something of a sinister look about it. Dark, with long shadows. Mostly because Walter had uttered the name "Maxwell Ross." And now, that name had Tom thinking that if something criminal was afoot in Sullivan, he needed to protect his daughter.

He had only been back to the old address once. Last Christmas. Because cardinals had swooped through the Sullivan sky, all in a single red blanket. He'd watched as they seemed to head in the direction of his former neighborhood.

Tom had hurried, fearful, not sure what it all meant. But when he'd arrived at the house and looked through the window, there she'd been. Geena. Typing away at her computer. Smiling. Laughing. Squealing every so often. An antique bottle sitting on the coffee table, next to her laptop.

He had smiled. *Love isn't only for the young*, he'd tried to tell her during their last Ruby's Place visit. Of course it wasn't. There it was. Love. In all sorts of forms and shades. Flashing across her face as she wrote.

The night had swallowed him as he'd turned to leave her in peace.

Now, though, Tom raced through the living room. He lunged for the writing desk, threw open the bottom drawer, and there it was: the manuscript. And the antique bottle Gee-na'd had beside her as she wrote.

Even in the bluish, hazy moonlight, he could see it— the mistletoe.

But there was no liquor left.

A familiar panic enveloped him. The same mind-bending fear he'd felt hit his bloodstream every time Geena had run a fever or been ten minutes late meeting curfew. He raced up the stairs to sit on the edge of Geena's bed.

"Did you drink all of it?" he murmured as she slept. She looked as peaceful at that moment as she had as a baby in her crib.

If she'd drunk it all, what could it still do? She didn't appear ill. Had she downed the entirety of it last winter? Why hadn't he recognized the bottle as Maxwell's? What if it infect-ed her with Maxwell's hatred? Is that what "poison" meant? When would that start to show?

Walter had infused Tom with questions for which there simply were no answers.

"Oh, Geena," Tom said quietly, touching her hair. "There's no magic in that bottle. Is that why you drank it? Why would you chance hurting yourself? What was so im-portant?"

But what could he do, other than watch over her? Other than hope?

Just as in years past, the watching would be torture.

Maybe even more so now. Because touching her hair no longer woke her up. He and Geena were in the same room and two separate worlds.

Tom crossed to the window. And on one of the stars situated right above Ruby's Place, he made a wish.

But in the way of Sullivan, that wish did not land for good on a star. And it did not stay a wish.

It turned into a request.

A cardinal touched down on a phone line and felt it buzz beneath his feet.

Geena

Early in the morning, a knock rattled my front door.

"Got indication that there's been issues at this address," a telephone technician insisted from his spot on the porch. The same man I'd repeatedly seen on the square, in coveralls, shimmying up telephone poles.

"You did? I didn't call to report a problem," I said.

"Got a request from a Tom," the technician informed me.

"Oh, see, his name was originally on the phone bill. I—"

"Need to check your setup inside," the technician insisted.

"I haven't noticed anything wrong," I said, even as I was backing up, letting the man inside.

"Been town-wide problems, ma'am. Best to check. Besides, I got this repair ticket last night. Emergency case."

"Emergency? I suppose. Town-wide, eh? I've been seeing you around," I blubbered. "The phone's in—"

But he'd already made a beeline for the dividing point

between the living room and the kitchen, where the downstairs phone and the answering machine had always been. Where I'd twisted the curly cord around my finger and listened to Rob's sweet teenage voice.

"Your answering machine isn't quite set up right," he observed.

"It's not?"

And then a new thought came to me, one that brought a frantic flush to my face. "There's a greeting message on that machine I was trying to save. The voice on it..."

"No worries, ma'am," he said, and for some reason, an intense feeling of calm washed over me.

I watched, quietly, but had barely had a chance to get a good look at the giant cardinal on the back of his coveralls—or wonder when it was that the local phone company had changed its logo—when he dropped his screwdriver back into his toolbelt.

"That should do it," he said, nodding a goodbye, and hurried back out the front door.

"Do—what?" I wondered, my brain slowly catching up.

I peeked out the window, expecting to find him on one of the telephone poles across the street.

He wasn't, though. No technician, no truck.

I edged back through the living room, tentatively reaching for the receiver. A dial tone buzzed in my ear. The machine flashed one unheard message, when it hadn't before. I pressed "Play" and listened to the silly, made-up message I'd placed from Iowa for my dad: "Hey, it's me. Just calling to let you know I'll be on the road as soon as I get my last grades turned in. See you soon."

I shrugged, replacing the receiver.

Company was coming. The sudden switch in thoughts made me the closest thing to happy I'd been since coming home.

Only a few days separated me from Chris's arrival, a fact I welcomed gladly. Time had been plodding along since I'd arrived in Sullivan, each day like a footstep in the snow—the sad, sloppy kind with mud and leaves stuck to it. A lonely feeling had started to settle into my chest, as unfamiliar to me as it was uncomfortable.

I'd already taken up the old master bedroom as my own, redecorating it, moving out some of Dad's hyper-masculine leather everything and replacing it with some white wicker furniture and yellow floral patterned bedding. Now that Chris would soon be on his way, I tackled Dad's reading room and what had been my own girlhood bedroom.

I'd long since taken down the posters for the hair metal bands of my youth (though part of me almost wished I'd kept a few—what falls out of fashion is bound to be vintage and cool in another year or two). Hung the new curtains I'd bought. Set out fresh bedding and towels and soap, too, all with the hope that maybe Chris might help brighten up the holiday. Nothing like a friend to make the world look like a different place, suddenly.

Hopefully, anyway.

When he showed up—on Christmas Eve, like he'd promised—I threw myself into the role of happy host. Met him in the driveway before he could so much as think about ringing the doorbell.

"Welcome," I bellowed.

But his was the smile usually found painted on plastic Santa faces. "So. This is Sullivan," he said, letting his car door slam shut.

"Don't make up your mind on first impressions," I warned. "It's more than just a small town."

"So you've said," Chris muttered, his eyes wandering over toward Mrs. Cranston, who was standing on her step cursing the front door that had grown sticky in the cold. He grimaced, his hand wandering back toward the driver's side door pull.

"Oh, no. You don't already regret it, do you?" I asked.

"Listen, Barister, it's just—I don't know about going tonight. To Ruby's."

"You do regret it!" I knocked my glasses higher up on my nose.

"I didn't tell you everything. About Christmas."

"Oh, man, you aren't going to tell me that engagement of yours ended on Christmas, are you?"

He sighed.

"You are." I put both hands on the top of my head, almost like I did when I was practicing duck and cover moves in elementary school.

I noticed he still hadn't locked his door. Or made a move to tug his bag from the trunk.

"You're here. I set up a room for you. Just please come inside," I said.

He considered it.

"You don't want to. I can tell."

"You can tell," he muttered.

"I've learned plenty sharing that hole-in-the-wall office with you. In fact, I'd say…" My voice trailed as I leaned forward to breathe him in. "Seven, maybe eight cigarettes. Two large cups of gas station coffee."

He appeared startled. Like I'd shaken him out of a daydream.

"What you need is an evening at Ruby's Place," I told him. "Cures what ails ya."

"That's the thing. I don't think it will."

"Maybe it's what *I* need," I confessed. "Maybe I need you here. Can I talk to you about something?"

"I don't know if I can take anything heavy."

"I might have written something."

"Uh-huh," he said, wagging a finger at me. "I knew it. You're trying to con me into an editorial job. On a holiday, no less."

"Just come on," I said. Before he could change his mind, I had both hands against his back, and I was pushing him up the front walk.

"Where is this masterpiece, anyway?" he asked, laughing as he flopped into Dad's old living room chair.

"I don't think I can show it to anybody yet," I admitted.

"Going to be one tough editorial job." He tugged his arms free from his coat. "Can't say I've ever edited something I wasn't allowed to read. What is this all about, anyway, Barister?"

"I mean—can I ask you about that?" I pointed to the small notebook poking out of his shirt pocket.

"Thought you already did. It's for my stories. The ones I collect. You know that."

"Why do you do it?"

"You mean since it's not for publication. What's the point. Right?"

I shrugged, nodded.

"Because it's a special thing when somebody shares their story with you. Even if it's a tiny sliver of it. A paragraph or two. Some silly anecdote. When somebody shares their story, they're asking you to see them. And by writing it down, I say I did."

"That's it?"

He nodded.

"That's not it. I can tell."

"Okay, officemate," he grumbled. "Here's the thing: I think the act of writing a story down has power."

"You do."

"Yes. Absolutely. Putting something down in print. It's magic."

"Magic."

"*Yes*, officemate." Chris leaned forward. "When I write some silly little story down, I feel like I'm having a conversation with the world. Like I've pointed out something it has to listen to. Writing it down makes the world pay attention. It's—well, I hate the cheap pun, but by writing it down, I've made it noteworthy. And sometimes, every so often, I can feel the world changing just a little bit because of what I've written."

"Even if no one has read it."

"Aren't you listening to me? By writing it, the world has heard it."

I frowned.

"Look, it's magic. It's not supposed to be easily understood." He offered a crooked grin.

"You're probably starved, and I have nothing to offer you to eat," I admitted. "I'd planned on us eating at Ruby's Place. I think Angela's having another prime rib dinner this year."

"Angela."

"The owner. Remember, I told you? Angela Lowe?"

Some new emotion flickered across Chris's face—but I couldn't quite figure it out. Surprise? New interest? He frowned, tugging on his bottom lip as he thought something out a moment. "I need to do something first. Why don't I meet you there?"

I was taken aback. He needed to run some sort of errand in a town he'd never been to before? "Do you need directions? To Ruby's?"

"Nah," he said, throwing his coat back on again. "On the square, right?" He grinned. "See you tonight, officemate."

And then he was gone. It hit me that he could actually disappear for good. After all, he'd never dragged his bags inside. In an hour or two, I might very well get a text saying he had decided to head somewhere else for the holiday. Along with some other flimsy excuse. Probably something about not wanting to barge in on my own Christmas Eve with Rob, even though I'd already assured him he wouldn't.

The more I considered it, the more likely it seemed. I felt a little embarrassed, actually. Like somebody who had wanted to throw a party, only to find no one had showed.

But I couldn't get what he'd said about stories—and the magic of writing something down—out of my mind...

I crossed to Dad's writing table. Took out a fresh sheet of paper. And scrawled:

Dear Dad,

I need to talk to you.

Love,
Geena

I chuckled at myself. "Magic in the written word," I grumbled.

I tossed my pen down. When I swiveled in the opposite direction from the writing desk, there he was. Sitting in the chair that Chris had filled just a moment ago. Legs crossed, a book in his hand, as I had seen him a million times before.

"Hey, Geenie," Dad said softly.

Geena

"How—what?" I took off my glasses and rubbed my eyes, feeling like a kid waking up from a dream. "Did I bring you here?" I asked, showing him the letter I'd just written.

Dad smiled at me. The same look I'd seen bringing him an A on my algebra test, or a stack of acceptance letters to grad schools, or, in later years, announcing I'd snagged a teaching contract. A real university professor.

It was that familiar dad look of pride.

"What?" I asked again. "I got something right. Didn't I? But what?"

He leaned back into his chair. Settled into all the bumps and grooves and crevices his body had pressed into that old recliner of his. He was once again a handsome young man—even younger than I was right then—with the dark hair and mustache I remembered him wearing when he was putting together my Big Wheel or anchoring my swing set in the backyard. And he was wearing his favorite flannel shirt, the one with the giant tear in the right elbow. The same shirt I hadn't been able to get rid of when I'd cleaned out the rest of his personal things, the one I had carefully wrapped in tissue and placed in my own dresser drawer. As if readying himself to answer my disjointed questions, he stuck a finger into the paperback he was holding to mark his place.

"Another Western?" I asked.

"I needed something to bide my time."

"What for?"

"I've been waiting."

"What—here? You've been here?"

"Yep."

"How long? But what about Ruby's? And you said—"

"I know what I told you. That we'd never see each other again."

"But that wasn't true. All this time, we could have—"

"I didn't get your message right away," he said, gesturing toward the answering machine. "Think I needed somebody to goose the old thing."

"My message?" The one I'd left while still in Iowa. The game I'd played in my mind about telling Dad I'd be coming home soon. I shivered a bit, remembering the technician in the coveralls who had recently come to the house.

"Came as soon as I heard it," Dad said.

"So you've been here a few days."

"Oh, I may have been by the house a couple of times before," Dad admitted. "But when I got your message and heard your voice reaching out to me...There was something in the tone. I knew you needed to talk to me. I also knew if you had reason to believe, you'd see me so that I could help you. Your friend gave you that a moment ago." He gestured toward my note.

"And that—it let me see you again?"

He shrugged. "Here we are," he said simply.

"There's more to it."

"Walter may have warned me something was amiss in Sullivan. He might have called on me."

"He needed help. From the police?"

"I'm not sure what I can do. It's not so simple anymore. What laws are being broken? I'm the one breaking the rules by being here. You know all about that, though. Don't you? The regulars at Ruby's Place. And Christmas Eve meetings with long-lost loved ones. You and I aren't the only people lucky enough to have had that."

"Did you read *my* book?" I asked, pulling the stack of pages into my lap. "Or the start of a book, anyway? The one I tried to write?"

"You know I'm a sucker for a good story," he said, holding up his paperback.

"Did I—did—"

"Gotten yourself into something of a jam." He pointed toward my manuscript.

"Yeah. I couldn't finish it," I grumbled.

"Why?"

"Because—I didn't know how to end it. No possibility seemed right."

"Why?"

"*Because.*"

He raised an eyebrow.

"I left so much story out. Okay? I told this tiny little

fraction. One person's always story, when..."

A new thought arrived, making me shiver. I flopped down on the floor in front of him—as I had so many times—to listen to him read story after story when I was a girl. Stories that filled my heart and mind—making me who I'd become.

"Stories," I repeated, pressing the side of my head against his knee. "Our *stories* are important. What we share with each other. I told Angela's story because I was so focused on a place. On the bar. But Ruby's Place isn't what's magical. It's us. Our stories.

"Our loved ones—the truly important souls we share our lives with—they're always with us. We need the wonder of the holiday to remind us of that. But it's possible to connect with them all year long, if we'd only hang on to our belief. That's it, isn't it?"

When I craned my neck to look up at him, Dad's face held that unforgettable grin again.

"I got everything wrong. My whole manuscript. Words do have power. Chris was right about that. I have to fix this," I said, snatching up my Pendleton jacket and hugging my pages to my chest. "I need to see Ruby."

"Nope," Dad said, dog-earring a page in his paperback. He stood and tossed the book into his chair. "You need to see Walter."

Geena

The late afternoon was growing hazy, Christmas Eve sliding ever closer toward sunset as Dad and I raced to the bank. With each step, I hugged my pages tighter and the ancient bottle I'd found the year before banged a little harder against my thigh. I'd shoved it yet again in the side pocket of my old gray wool coat. I wasn't sure what an empty container could do, but I didn't think I should leave it behind, either.

Funny how hard I kept clinging to that old bottle. Maybe that's the way with things that come to us accidentally. Maybe we can't ever stop suspecting they come to us for a reason.

"I'll never get inside," I warned him. "Scott makes sure the place closes early."

Dad only grinned and took me down the alley, toward a door marked "Employees Only." He rapped against it, like we were customers waiting to get into Frankie's speakeasy. Three knocks—a pause—two knocks.

The door flew open. And there stood Walter—as if he'd been expecting us. I saw him as plainly as I saw Dad. He was real.

"I have it," I insisted, holding up my manuscript.

Walter looked over at Dad, who winked at him with reassurance.

"It's the answer," I insisted. "To everything. It's just got to be."

Walter backed up, letting me inside. I was chattering away the whole time. "I found a bottle," I told him.

Walter stopped short. "What kind of bottle?"

Dad smiled. "The one you were looking for."

Geena

"Did you drink from it?" Walter asked as I pulled the bottle from my coat pocket.

"I did. A little, anyway. The rest got poured out. But what I drank made me see everything. Last Christmas. I wrote it all down." I pushed my manuscript toward Walter. "I wrote everything I saw. And I think—whatever has happened to Sullivan, I think it's my fault. Words have power." I was struggling to put new information with what I already felt certain of. Somehow, the pieces were jagged, and still didn't quite fit.

"When did you begin to write your book?" he asked.

"It's not even close to a book," I corrected. "Just a few chapters. But I started last Christmas."

His eyes widened. "I found some people waiting in the lost and found."

"Lost and—"

"At Ruby's. There's a room filled with spirits. Who are in danger of being forgotten completely. When you wrote your story—"

"I wrote about Sullivan. Ruby's Place. And Angela.

And the regulars."

Walter seemed shocked. "You wrote about the regulars?"

"I wrote what I saw."

"You wrote memories." He grabbed my hand and started dragging me to the back of the bank. Dad followed less than a single footstep behind. "Come this way," Walter said. "I'm going to show you a vault that's as old as the town."

Dad and I watched as Walter spun the wheel. The door clanked open. The only item inside was a single large metal box.

He tugged it out, popped it open.

"It's empty," I said.

"It's where I keep the deposits. The memories of Sullivan. At the end of every single holiday season, I lock them safely away. This year, when I went to retrieve them, they were gone. I thought they'd been stolen."

"I did it, didn't I? I never meant to," I insisted.

"Don't you see?" Walter asked. "It's actually wonderful. Because it means the memories of Sullivan aren't gone. Just in a different place."

"We have to get them out of this thing," I said, flapping the pages. "What if I destroy it?"

"Are you sure?" Dad asked. "You've already put so much of yourself into it. Your own dreams. And what about your hopes for The Page Turner?"

I was surprised for a moment that he knew I'd dreamed of being able to help Rob. But then again—why wouldn't he know?

"But Dad," I started, "it wasn't my intention to ever hurt anybody. Erase their memories. Take away the Christmas spirit. If I go forward with it..." My voice trailed as a new thought came to me.

The bank grew quiet. The kind of quiet that had a hum.

"I saw the story of Sullivan when I drank from the bottle, but it showed me more than I could cram into one book—and also didn't quite show me everything. Not how it all tied together," I admitted. "I had to make leaps when I was writing. And I gave the power to Ruby's Place. But it wasn't about Ruby's at all. It was about us. All of us. Not ghosts. And it's not about regret, either. It's about love. All kinds of love— romantic, friendship, family...Love can never be a ghost. Love is always alive. I got that wrong, too."

"Maxwell Ross got it wrong," Walter corrected.

"Who?" I asked. Had I seen him the year before, in that flash? In the scenes from the past?

"He made the liquor in this bottle, didn't he?" I asked.

"Decades ago," Walter agreed. "With the idea that it could finally help him get even with a town that he felt had given him nothing but raw deals. The reason you got mixed up was because you were drinking the liquor he made. Revenge itself is a mixed-up desire."

I shook my head. "I really should have known better. I already learned that love never dies. It never ages. The love I had with Rob didn't. Even you hinted at that, the year I saw you in Ruby's," I said, looking at Dad.

"But it's *not* about Ruby's," I reminded myself. "Memories don't need an external place. Just like love doesn't exist in a single place or time. It's with us always. Ruby's isn't magical. Neither is Sullivan. It's us. It's our memories. Who we are to each other."

When they didn't answer, I insisted, again, "The story was wrong. I misinterpreted everything. And words have *power*."

Walter paced nervously, the metal box in his hand.

"I'm telling you, we have to get rid of this book," I repeated. "I know it. I'm so sorry."

I tossed the manuscript on a nearby table. I tore the top page off, crumpled it up in my hands, and tossed it into a wastebasket.

"Did that do anything?" I asked.

Walter and Dad glanced about. But nothing had changed. If only I'd seen the Memory Bank in the scenes from the bottle. If only I'd had some sort of clue that writing the wrong story could do damage.

I grabbed a pen from Walter's shirt pocket and scribbled out the first few lines on the next page.

"Anything?"

Water and Dad both shook their heads.

I'd twisted the story. And now that it was all mangled and messed up, I couldn't get it out of the pages again.

Frustrated, I threw the manuscript on the floor and stomped it.

"Geena," Walter whispered as he shoved Maxwell's old bottle under my nose.

The mistletoe inside was glowing. Almost as though

the berries were tiny little white twinkle lights.

I grabbed the bottle again. But I was shaking so much, the bottle slipped.

I screamed in fear. Maxwell's bottle had been tainted with revenge. What damage was it about to do?

The bottle tumbled, shattering against the floor. Glass pieces flew into the air, sparkling like water droplets. They evaporated before they could fall again.

The mistletoe tumbled onto my manuscript. In the light the berries cast, the words on my pages began to tremble.

We watched as words pulled free from the pages, buzzing into the air. They paused, hovering for a moment as if waiting for something.

Walter lurched into action, opening the metal box that he'd removed from the vault. The words flew inside. The lid clanked shut.

"They're back!" Walter shouted.

"The memories?" I asked.

"Quick," he told me. "Open the window."

I lunged forward and heaved. Cold air burst into the bank as I stepped to the side, clearing the way for whatever Walter had in mind.

Walter took a deep breath. He gingerly took hold of the lid of the metal box. He cracked it slightly. The room filled with the sound of flapping wings.

When Walter opened the box the rest of the way, out flew a huge chattering flock of cardinals. They chirped and squawked as they flapped their wings.

They began to sing in unison just before they soared

out of the window, obviously happy to be free.

Dad, Walter, and I pushed our heads outside to watch what would happen next.

Remember When...

The cardinals soared, gaining speed, all of them together in a flock. They hovered against the cold winter sky, long enough to cast a slight reddish glow—like a sunset warming the horizon. Just when it appeared they might well hang there indefinitely, they scattered, all in a single burst. Some headed south toward Sullivan's newest housing development, while others raced north, past the emptied, dark high school. Some landed on windowsills on the square. Others landed on car hoods or near entrances of stores like the It Ain't Over Yet. Several flew toward the Senior Center around the corner.

Those at the back of the flock raced to one of Sullivan's oldest neighborhoods. Two swooped toward a couple of homes a block away from Geena's mother's old house. They flittered in front of the same bungalows Rob and Geena had once parked in front of, as teenagers, exchanging Christmas gifts behind the steamy windows of Rob's Caprice.

"Scat!" Pamela Krunk shouted at the bird who began flapping his wings in her face. She waved her hands furiously, trying to frighten him away.

"What's wrong with you? Get!" she ordered, as her dog Rufus began to bark as well, seeming every bit as annoyed.

The cardinal offered a few more flaps—for good measure, it almost seemed—before taking off, heading for an oak tree branch.

"I never!" Pamela grumbled. But when she lowered her arms, she found her neighbor, Susan Fitzweather, standing in her own front yard, a fresh pine garland in her hand. Pamela's heart suddenly swelled with all the memories of December coffee cake at Susan's kitchen table, the times they both walked the snowy neighborhood with Rufus, the stories they had shared during brief intervals at their chain-link fence as they'd dashed into backyards to grab new logs for their fires or brought the dog out for the umpteenth time.

Why, she and Susan were friends. Not just neighbors. Anything that had ever stood between them had been like that old chain-link—full of gaping holes. Hadn't they always been able to see each other? And hadn't seeing each other always been a comfort? Hadn't it felt like the world's greatest security to Pamela, knowing that Susan was ten feet away?

Pamela's face softened, erasing her scowl. The nearby cardinal chirped happily.

"You still putting up your decorations?" Pamela called out, pointing to the garland. It was all she could think of. Her voice, for the first time since the start of the holiday season, was soft. Kind. She wondered why it had taken her so long to get to this feeling. How could she have forgotten how important their friendship had always been to her?

"I—was taking them down," Susan admitted. She

touched her own forehead, unsure why she had spent so many weeks racing inside each time she saw her neighbor, scurrying away before Pamela could wave or say hello. Unsure why she had worked so hard to avoid having to say hello back. "So close to Christmas, I thought I'd get a head start," Susan went on. "But it's not even Christmas yet. Why would I do that?"

Suddenly, Susan was remembering her husband's retirement party last year, and how she and Pamela had tiptoed off to the back step of the rented dance hall together. How Pamela had given her a gift of her own—a kind of gag sympathy gift now that her husband would be home all the time. How special it had felt to have someone there with her, who could elbow her in the ribs and make her feel less like something enormous had come to an end. How the night had felt special and sweet and lovely beside Pamela.

"You going to Ruby's?" Susan called out. "It is Christmas Eve."

"I wasn't, but—tell you what, why don't I walk Rufus, and then the two of us can head down there and see what's going on?"

"Why don't we walk together?" Susan suggested. "We haven't done that in a while."

"I'd love that," Pamela said.

Susan smiled, draping her garland around her "Welcome to Christmas" sign. Pamela laughed, feeling lighter and happier than she had in ages.

Closer to the square, one of the last straggling cardinals to make it out of the Memory Bank landed on a phone line. The slight weight of his body made ripples travel the length of the line, all the way to the It Ain't Over Yet.

Inside the flea market, the old switchboard lit up. Voices began to pour out of the headset.

Tina froze, her hand on the cash register she had been in the midst of locking up.

"Hello?" she asked.

And still, the voices poured, getting increasingly louder, each one of them struggling to be the one to be heard. "Rose?" they kept asking. "Rose! You there?"

Tina had just started out from behind the counter when she saw him. The phone technician, the one who had been scrambling up telephone poles all across the square. He was standing outside her business now, waving from the other side of the plate glass, smiling at her before turning away, flashing the giant redbird logo on the back of his coveralls.

She blinked, and the technician disappeared completely. In his place, a cardinal sat perched on the windowsill. He flapped his wings before being absorbed by a large flock of cardinals swooping by.

They soared ever higher, swirling into the alley behind Ruby's. Zipping straight through the bullet holes along the ancient back door.

One of them emerged in the lost and found. With Rose's headset in his beak.

Rose stood. Trembling, she asked, "Do I dare try it?"

Frankie only stared at her wide-eyed.

The cardinal swooped for the door.

Rose held her arm through the opening.

And she did not disappear.

Rose raced out of the bar, back toward the It Ain't Over Yet, the cold air tingling against her.

She arrived at the flea market only to find Tina seated in front of the switchboard, cords in her hand, trying to chase down the flashing lights.

Rose nudged her. "Scoot," she said.

Tina flinched, lunging from the chair.

With her headset on, Rose started making connections. All over town.

Perhaps most importantly, she connected to the history museum.

***

Linda Bryant wasn't sure what she was even doing anymore.

She had been through the contents of the Sullivan History Museum more times than she could count. *Panning for gold*, that was how Toby had phrased it.

But she had not been able to get Geena's voice out of her mind. Asking her to keep at it.

Keep at what? What was she looking for? What would help the museum? Interest Sullivanites again?

As she wondered, in the relatively dark and still museum, the bottom drawer of the Ruby's Place cabinet began to rattle. It shook like a lid on a boiling pot. Like something was about to blow.

Linda slowly made her way toward the cabinet, which only continued to rattle and tremble.

She grabbed the handle on the bottom drawer and

threw it open.

Pictures and papers flew out, into the air.

She yelped, immediately scrambling to gather them up again.

But they continued to fly out of the drawer, page after page, story after story, document after document, flipping about like cards from a deck being shuffled.

The nearby window flew open.

Linda cried out in horror as the pictures and pages all blew outside. All those years, all those stories. Somehow, in the span of only a few seconds, had she really lost everything that Toby had preserved for their town?

The sound of a ringing phone began to echo through what suddenly felt like a very empty museum.

But where was it coming from? The history museum's phone was downstairs, in Toby's office. Somewhere in the back of her foggy brain, it occurred to Linda to look back into the bottom drawer.

The images and stories were gone, but the old candlestick phone remained—the same phone that had once been inside Ruby's, that had connected Frankie to Ludlow, her liquor supplier.

And it was ringing.

Linda placed the earpiece against her head. "Hello?"

"It's me. Rose," the voice insisted through the earpiece. "Don't worry. Those donations didn't disappear. They're not gone. Just the opposite.

"Hurry," Rose insisted. "You need to get to Ruby's Place."

***

All across town, cardinals flapped their wings, scattering warm memories. Making hearts swell with love, with affection, with all the joy Christmas can bring.

Neighbors began knocking on neighbors' doors. Phones were ringing. Kimberly Tan drove out to the florist shop where she worked and filled her car with all the poinsettias the people of Sullivan were not buying. She instantly began a delivery route—to nearby nursing homes and churches.

As the sound of fluttering wings began to soften, voices once more filled the air: "Do you remember—?" and "I haven't thought of that Christmas in ages," or "I wonder how she's doing?"

Bedroom dresser drawers slid open. Hands darted through jewelry boxes, searching for that special holiday pin. Suit jackets were being pulled from closets, inspected for wrinkles. Suddenly, fathers were showing sons how to tie their neckties while mothers were curling their daughters' hair, sharing perfume and cologne.

Everyone jumped into their cars and they came back— to the square. And Ruby's.

Parking spaces quickly filled outside of the old bar. And then filled the lot at the bank. Cars spilled over into neighboring streets, where passersby swung their arms about, laughing as they helped drivers parallel park. Radios were tuned to holiday music. Windows were rolled down and arms stuck through the openings as celebrators waved to each other. Horns honked cheerful hellos.

"Come on, Mom!" little ten-year-old Maddie screeched. She grabbed her mother's hand. "It's going to be even better than last year. Remember? When I played that song for you?"

"I do. Best 'Jingle Bells' ever performed," her mother agreed.

"I'm going to play it again." Maddie placed her cheek against her mother's arm.

"This time, we can sing together," her mother corrected.

They raced each other to get in line outside of the familiar bright green door. To feel the warmth of the Ruby's Place red neon glow.

***

"Can you believe that crowd?" Geena asked, still standing at the window in the bank. When no one answered, she glanced behind her shoulder. The bank was empty around her. Somehow, though, Geena didn't feel alone. She turned back toward the street below—the cars, the streams of revelers.

Though her spot gave her a perfectly unobstructed view of Sullivan, Geena couldn't bear to stay. She had to be part of what was happening. She raced outside, into the square. She could feel the magic of the memories she had given back to her hometown. Everyone's always story trickled through the air. She began to turn circles, like a little girl marveling at a snowstorm.

All around her, the past and present were mingling. Tidbits from their shared history—the faces from the bottom drawer of the Ruby's Place cabinet in the history museum—had returned. Most endings, after all, were merely pauses. Bookmarked pages just waiting for the moment when someone who knew the story's beginning would return, open the volume again.

The door to the It Ain't Over Yet jingled closed as Tina began to make her way down the sidewalk, wearing a 1930s-era old Hollywood evening gown under a black wool coat with a fur collar and cuffs. And a couple of items from her display case back at the shop: the Eisenberg pin and the cloche hat.

Geena's eyes widened as a woman emerged from Ruby's Place with a sandwich board bearing a simple "Merry Christmas!" A large woman, Geena noted. One who nodded hellos when others greeted her with the name "Frankie."

The lost and found was no longer holding prisoners. Because those who had been drawn to Ruby's were yet again sharing their stories—those they had lived, and those they had inherited. With their names on lips and in minds and hearts, the figures from the lost and found were lost no more. The stories themselves had claimed them.

"Excuse me," a woman pleaded, pushing her way outside of Ruby's as everyone else was trying to push their way in. Geena recognized her instantly from the picture that had always hung behind the bar. In fact, she was wearing the very same ivory sateen performing gown she had donned for the photo. The woman hurried through the crowd, bobbing and weaving and letting out the occasional "Ooomph!" or "Pardon me. Excuse me," until she found Tina.

"If you don't mind," Dorothy said, "that's mine. I've been looking for it everywhere." And she snatched the cloche right off of Tina's head.

Geena laughed at the scene. It seemed to her at that moment that memory powered everything: love and sentimentality and hope.

And belief. It seemed to her that a strong memory of lovely times fueled the belief that a future filled with good things could be possible.

The giggles were still pouring out of her even as she heard her name. "Geena!" Rob was shouting, running toward her. Without hesitation, he swept her up in his arms, giving her the hug and the kiss that she had expected upon her return home.

"Oh, what an incredible holiday," he said. "I'm so glad you're here. I was about to head to your place. This is such a great Christmas. Isn't it? Almost as good as the one before I left for the service. Remember? How we spent it nearly freezing to death in my car? Couple of crazy kids."

Geena laughed. "I do—why do you think I wear this ugly thing?" she asked, clutching the nail on a chain he had given her that year.

"And it felt like we were the only two people in the world? Just you and me."

She nodded. "Yes!" She laughed again, this time at the delightful feeling of knowing Rob's memories were merging with her own. It was, she suspected, the best present this

Christmas would give her—knowing she was part of Rob's own always story.

"Let's have another," he said. "A private Christmas Eve. The two of us."

"Not even go to Ruby's?"

"After Ruby's. After helping out Angela, like we promised."

"You won't be dead tired?"

"I'm never going to sleep again." He held up a book, but in the haze of the streetlights, she couldn't quite see what it was. "I found this in your dad's box."

Geena shook her head, not understanding. He pulled out his cell and shined a light. "Look," he insisted.

"*East of Eden*," she read.

"Go to the copyright page."

"First edition," she sighed.

"Title page."

"Signed." Geena staggered a little. Her mouth drooped. Her eyes went wide. She felt like a stand-in for someone receiving a six-figure appraisal on *Antiques Roadshow*.

She didn't remember even putting that book in the box. "Dad," she whispered. He'd slipped it in. She couldn't know how, exactly, but it had to be him. She was sure of it.

"You're going to make so much money on this thing," Rob said. "I can't wait. We've got to call some big auction house. Sotheby's, maybe! First thing—"

"No," Geena interrupted.

"No?"

"No—I don't want it. I gave it to you. For the store.

Besides, where do you think Dad got it? I bet you sold it to him in the first place—gave him first look at some estate sale box, maybe. It wouldn't have mattered to you if you got a ton of money for it—not if you were selling it to Dad. Probably the only reason you ever took his money at all was as a sign of respect for him. Make sure he didn't think you were somehow pandering to him."

"But it was your dad's. I couldn't—"

"*For the store*," Geena repeated, in a way that said she knew what dire straits he was facing.

He reached up to tuck her hair behind her ear. He held her gaze for a moment before flashing a wide smile and bellowing out a "Merry Christmas!" He was laughing as he grabbed her into his arms again.

As they embraced, Sullivan's stories continued to swirl around them.

"Let's lock up," he said, urging her toward The Page Turner. "Come on. Thanks to you, I kind of feel like everything in the world suddenly got fixed."

She took a step and stopped. Grabbed Rob's hand. "Look," she said, pointing to their sidewalk. The square with their names—the one that had appeared cracked earlier—had inexplicably mended, looking as though Rob's declaration of love had been carved earlier that very day.

Welcome To Ruby's Place

Angela wiped a tear from her eye.

They were back. All of them. The current Sullivan residents and the regulars both. The bar was full of Christmas spirits and those who had come to find that spirit again.

Dorothy leaned against the piano as a trumpet wailed. Chester moved forward, the white metal of his instrument catching the light.

Tina staggered. She'd had that trumpet in her front window display. Hard not to recognize it with all that intricate carving.

It was coming back to her now. Rose, she remembered, had worked her switchboard magic last year. Summoned the original owner.

Chester had arrived, begging Tina to let him work enough hours at her shop to earn that trumpet. "I promised my love I'd come back on Christmas Eve," he'd said. "I told her I'd come for her. I can't go to her, though, without my music."

They had reunited last Christmas. Tina had seen it.

Witnessed the full power of their love. Felt it in their melodies. Even though their story was nearly a hundred years old.

She felt herself tearing up. Old objects, she thought, eyeing the trumpet and Dorothy's cloche hat, really *were* powerful.

Then again, so were old bars.

Just ask Toby over at the history museum.

The door behind Tina burst open again and again. Linda arrived, breathless. So did Kimberly Tan. And Pamela Krunk and her friend Susan. The joy that they brought danced and clustered about the bar. That joy helped pull back chairs and pushed tables together. It leaned against the piano to sing another chorus.

And still, outside, the sidewalk was crammed full of people dressed in their finest, slowly snaking their way closer, wanting to get in before midnight passed and Christmas Eve had become Christmas day.

Angela took in a deep breath, finding the air smelling of prime rib dinners and cocoa. Her open door added so many festive smells—snow and chimney smoke and even, she imagined, the perfume on the skin of the customers still standing outside, waiting to get in. Maybe, she thought, that perfume wasn't exactly high dollar. Maybe a heel or two had globs of glue holding soles on or strips of leather together. Maybe a coat had a hole, stitched with thread that didn't quite match. But it was still for Angela a display far more elegant— more festive—than any Hollywood red carpet.

Inside, Ruby worked every bit as tirelessly as Angela, helping her rattle ice through her cocktail shaker. But she was not Angela's only help.

"No shortcuts!" Frankie bellowed, insisting on using their own simple syrup, on including fresh mint, being picky about which lime wedges were chosen to spear onto glass rims, insisting anything bruised or damaged got tossed.

Angela chuckled, listening.

But she had also learned, over the last few years, that mastering cocktails meant you really did have to get every last ingredient right. Something a little bitter, something a little sweet—the perfect balance. Without it, a favorite cocktail could become undrinkable. And on Christmas Eve, the ingredient that made the atmosphere of Ruby's Place a perfect concoction was the fact that everyone inside saw with their hearts, making the unbelievable perfectly plausible.

As she stood, a cardinal swooped toward her front window. The creature landed on the sill for a moment before fluttering off again. Angela smiled, remembering her own first night at the bar, back when she was a little girl. That cardinal, it seemed, had brought her old memory back, in vivid detail. The sadness in her heart. The icy cold of the back step seeping through her dress as she sat, listening to Dorothy's story.

This Christmas Eve would be complete, she thought—if only…

She waved Geena to the bar. "You okay with mixing drinks for a few minutes?" she asked, reaching beneath the counter to retrieve that old, ugly brown hat.

Hands shaking, Angela carried two cups of cocoa toward the table in the back.

But she stopped. A man was already seated there.

No! Angela wanted to shout. Something about this Christmas felt different. Closer to the original Christmases of Angela's youth. Closer to her old always story. The one that had not yet come to its happy ending. For a minute there, she'd had such hopes about seeing her sister again. And now, some stranger was filling Gail's seat. Should she tell him? Kick him out?

Maybe, she thought, it would be best to come back later. Even though it would be torture to wait.

As she turned, the man cried out, "Angela!"

She swiveled again. How did he know her name? Had one of the customers told him?

But then he grinned, and she saw it: the scar along his jaw. The result of the sledding accident. The two of them trying to make it down Old Scroggin's Mountain, finding out just a little too late that two adults were too big for a single sled. They had fallen, and he had cut himself, and they had gone to the emergency room rather than Ruby's Place like they'd intended.

Next Christmas, they should have promised each other. But as the night spiraled far from their original plans, there had been an argument. The kind of argument that had the power to change everything—and the kind of argument about such strange, fragile fears that it was hard to remember all the details, explain what had happened to their families.

All that either one of them knew was that they never did make it into the city limits of Sullivan. Just one of thousands of plans they'd made that were never going to happen.

"Chris," Angela said. The Chris she had once believed—as the love songs proclaimed—held the moon and all the stars. The same Chris whose life she had once intended to share.

Angela's mind swarmed with a wild mix of thoughts and feelings. He had aged, but somehow, her memories of him were just as young as ever. They felt close, like events that had happened a handful of nights ago.

She placed the tray on the table and sat down, not knowing what else to say.

His grin widened. "I hope you don't mind. I hope I'm not crashing your Christmas party."

"Of course you're not. Anyone can come," she said, then regretted how it sounded.

"That's for you," Chris offered, pushing a clumsily wrapped package closer to her.

Angela's head spun as she opened it. "It's fruitcake."

"It's ridiculous, I know," Chris laughed. "On the edge of town, I stopped to fill the tank, and a woman at the gas station told me about them. Said she made them. I bought one for you. It used to make you think of your sister. Remember? I'd buy one, and we'd sit at the tiny little table in your apartment, and you'd tell me stories about Gail. About her track stuff, or the music she listened to, or her favorite red sweater."

"Neither one of us ever ate the stuff."

"But it made you tell me stories."

"Yeah."

"I loved that you told me those stories," Chris said, touching the top of his small pocket notebook for a moment.

"Funniest thing," he admitted. "I came to Sullivan to

see a friend of mine. We work together. I said I'd stay for Christmas, but—I knew you were here, and I had second thoughts. I was about to leave town again, when a cardinal came and landed on my car—the guy just wouldn't leave. And as I was staring at him, I got this flood of—maybe nostalgia. Suddenly, I couldn't leave town without seeing you. Just—the old times were so strong, and…Anyway, I went back to the gas station, and bought one of her cakes, hoping you'd tell me about Gail again."

Angela laughed, wiping a tear from the corner of her eye.

"Maybe," Chris said, offering her a fork, "if you're so inclined, you'd even tell me a few stories about yourself."

Angela leaned closer, propping her elbows on the table. As she spoke, the air around them filled with yet another scattering of memories. It was all coming back. Every last moment.

At the bar, Geena elbowed Rob and nodded once toward the table in the back. "Look at that," she said. "My friend Chris isn't as much of a stranger to all things Sullivan as he tried to make himself out to be." She supposed this was what Chris hadn't quite been able to talk about with her, what had been behind the guardrails he'd installed around his past.

Now, though, happy endings began to bloom in both Rob's and Geena's imaginations. Perhaps, for Chris and Angela, this would be a single sweet evening—the kind of perfect night with the power to heal a scar for good. Or perhaps their happy ending would not be an ending at all, but a new beginning. The start of a long-lasting relationship, one not unlike that which Rob and Geena had found themselves. A second shot at romance. A couple older and wiser in the ways of love.

Rob squeezed Geena's hand. She leaned in close to kiss his cheek.

The piano thundered. Voices rose. The entire bar bellowed the chorus of "We Wish You a Merry Christmas." Shiny wrapping was shredded from boxes. Ribbon fluttered to the ground. Mistletoe appeared.

And in the spaces between each one of the people who had raced to Ruby's, unexpected figures appeared. Easy to see them now that memories had been refreshed. Eyes opened in shock. Hands rested on chests in attempts to steady racing hearts. Overwhelmed, young and old Sullivanites staggered forward, each one throwing their arms around one of Ruby's after-hour regulars. The spirit, the face of their own Christmases past. "It's you. I can't believe it's you," rippled through the air.

Walter appeared at the edge of the bar, picking up his scotch neat. He raised the glass as though to offer a toast to Geena.

But Geena was busy pouring a pint. Unseen by her, a man in a flannel shirt appeared, a well-dressed beauty at his side.

A slender woman with a bun slipped between Geena and Rob.

"Another successful year, Rubes," Walter told her.

She beamed. All around them, Christmas music played behind unexpected meetings and the shrieks of happiness—rhythmically, it seemed, like the beat of a heart.

Any bitterness or anger or misunderstandings evaporated, leaving only laughter.

Christmas was once again alive in Sullivan.

As the Story Fades to Black...

What, exactly, *is* the truth of Sullivan?

Two possibilities have emerged.

Perhaps you believe that the story of Ruby's Place—and the incidents that have been described—are all quite literal. You believe that a gloomy Angela returned to town, and a cardinal (no, an angel, like the old saying, *cardinals appear when angels are near*) caused her to stop in front of the old bar. You believe she was pushed inside the derelict and long-closed Ruby's Place only to find it full of spirits. You also believe its ghosts get together during an after-hours happy hour each night. That once a year, on Christmas, the same spirits mingle with the living. Meetings take place. Hugs are exchanged along with messages of love. You believe that the ghost of the town's banker gathers up all the memories made that night, placing them for safekeeping in the Sullivan Memory Bank. And the next year, those memories are released to whisper in our ears. Urge us to climb into the backseats of cars. They tug at our hearts until we decide it really is a good idea to spend Christmas Eve at Ruby's.

Maybe you believe this story is about the possibility of having one last very real face-to-face meeting with a long-lost loved one—the ultimate Christmas gift.

Then again...

Perhaps you believe that the story of Sullivan—and Ruby's Place—is a metaphor for what it means to find Christmas. A metaphor for the power of memory.

If you believe it's a metaphor, you would also surely find it easy to believe that when Angela returned to town, she wasn't pushed inside the old bar. She broke in. The work wasn't hard, not with the padlock having grown so rusted and brittle. Stepping inside, she could feel it all around her—every memory of those Christmases with her aunt right there in the room with her.

But Angela wasn't the only one—not once the bar was officially open again. Having the old landmark back meant that stories crackled to life. Perhaps it was why Ruby's menu included marshmallows and cocoa. It wasn't just about offering a treat to satisfy the kids. It was a way to entice an adult to return to the sweetness of their own life, to recall the peaceful simplicity of that first winter snowfall—and Christmas lights, and maybe even the excitement Santa's arrival had once brought.

Last year, in the midst of all the sentimentalizing of the past, Geena really did stand on the sidewalk outside of Ruby's. Regardless of whether you think the entire story is literal or not, you can trust that much really did happen. It was midnight, the festivities all winding down, and she was waiting for Rob to finish his goodbyes to Angela. Christmas Eve had all but spun down to an end.

But if you believe this story is a metaphor, you would also believe that she did not find an antique bottle filled with liquor.

What would have happened?

The door opened. And Scott Drummond stepped outside.

"Hey, Gene," he said, shrugging himself into his coat.

"Didn't know you were still around," Geena said. "Getting to be something of a habit, you and me and Rob being the very last to leave." She was remembering the year before, how Scott had returned to Ruby's Place after putting the kids to bed. How he had not yet had enough of the majesty of the place. "Where's your wife?" She shivered. Snow was beginning to swirl like confetti in the streetlights.

"Bending Angela's ear." He wagged a thumb toward the door.

Geena nodded, the two of them looking through the front window.

"I'm so glad Angela got this place open again. It's really good for her."

"Good for all of us," Geena agreed. "Look how happy your wife is."

"Yeah, but especially Angela. This time of year used to be so hard for her."

"Why's that?" Geena shoved her hands into the deep side pockets of her wool coat. Her fingertips were already tingling painfully.

"Because of her sister. She died when Angela was just a

kid. I know she gets to missing her during the holidays. Misses her *something fierce* as some around here might phrase it."

He chuckled a bit, but Scott's face softened as he thought back. "Angela and I both used to come to Ruby's Place on Christmas Eve. I'd be with my dad, and she'd show up with her aunt. I remember Angela telling this story—'Later on,' she'd say, 'my sister's coming.' Like it was the only way to make it through the holiday. Even though we were all dressed up, and it was a big party, and it was Christmas, and we were happy, there was still something missing for her. She needed that made-up story. Needed to pretend that things were different for a little while."

"I had no idea," Geena said, watching through the window as Rob offered Angela a goodnight hug.

"I remember once, I ran into her at Ruby's when we were adults. Wasn't Christmas Eve, but we both happened to be there. I was with a date—can't remember her name now. It was so long ago—late '80s, maybe. But I remember Angela. She was so down. Maybe something was going wrong with that fiancé of hers. Or maybe it already had, they'd already broken up? So strange—all those things that are supposed to be so important fade. I just know it had been a long time since we'd seen each other. I doubted she remembered me—but she did. Remembered everybody, it turned out. My dad. The name of the piano player and the singer and—" Scott sighed.

"She told me," he went on, "I'll never forget it—said she wished there was a door someplace you could walk through. And your memories were on the other side. Right there, just waiting for you. And you could walk inside, and the past as you remembered it would be real again."

Hairs stood on the back of Geena's neck. *What if,* she began to think, *the bar wasn't just something that kept Angela busy, kept her from getting overly sad? What if the bright green door on the front of Ruby's really was that very magical doorway? What if it brought her sister to her? What if this place really did allow memories to come sit right beside you? Like I'd fantasized, the year Dad died, about getting one more chance to see him? What kind of comfort and wonder would Angela feel getting to see her sister's face? What if that was why she came back? What if that was why it was so important to her to buy the old place?*

Yes, if you believe this tale is a metaphor, you are certain there was never any literal bottle. The shot of liquor you previously watched her ingest was simply a symbol of what it feels like to be hit with a shot of inspiration.

You'd also readily believe that Geena really did race home and begin to write. Scribbling furiously. And then— eight chapters later—Geena simply hit a wall. She was unable to finish her manuscript. She could not see a way to end the story of what occurred in Ruby's Place on Christmas Eve.

Fast forward one year—to this year, this Christmas season—and Geena was in her office at the university. The end of the semester had arrived, and she was goading Chris into a visit. "You know you'd like to see it," she was saying. "Ruby's Place on Christmas Eve, I mean. The way I've talked it up? You have to be curious." In truth, she did want Chris to come fill up the empty rooms in her house, help distract her from her father's absence. But she also needed help with her book. She could not let the book go. Surely, she thought, there had to be a perfect ending in there somewhere. Maybe Chris, the story collector, could help her find it.

While there was hope in his acceptance of her invitation, she still could not shake her sadness, her discouragement regarding her writing, her displeasure with herself. So great were her sour feelings that it was not the town of Sullivan that was different when Geena returned home that winter—it was Geena that was different. The town's Memory Bank was not robbed. Sullivanites had not forgotten the feeling of Christmas—Geena had. Disappointed with herself and her inability to finish what she'd started, she found herself unable to see happiness in others.

When Chris arrived, she pointed to her father's old chair and handed him her pages. Instead of being able to provide some sort of editorial advice, though, he saw only Angela's name.

Yes, regardless of which version you believe—literal or metaphorical—Chris really was Angela's fiancé. Flooded with his own memories, it was suddenly imperative that he see his old love once again.

If you believe in the metaphorical version of this story, you'd see that Chris would make an excuse to leave, not able to stomach the idea of taking the time to explain who Angela had been to him. And Geena remained by herself in the house, waiting for Rob to arrive as promised, to pick her up for their Christmas Eve at Ruby's. In her bedroom, she stumbled upon the shirt she'd preserved that had belonged to her father—the old flannel thing with the torn elbow she hadn't quite been able to get rid of. The same way the Angela in Geena's story had not quite been able to get rid of her hat.

Geena slipped into her father's favorite flannel shirt. Rolling the sleeves, she headed downstairs. And she turned on a DVD of old home movies. Her dad became real again—or at least, the image of him did. There he was, joining her in the living room. His face flickering on her walls all around her.

And she knew—the real story, the one she should have written—wasn't about ghosts and cocktails and faces in the window of an old bar.

The real story was the one she had lived with her dad. He was her always story. The strong, enduring presence who really had sent her out to The Page Turner, only moments before his passing. The one who had steered her back to her Rob. *Love isn't only for the young*, he'd told her.

Neither were dreams.

She could see it—her book. It would come together quickly, she knew. After all, she'd been making up stories about her father for ages. Stitching them together in her head. Including the one about Elizabeth being his late-in-life love. Of course that had been made up. Why, the rumors of Elizabeth's movie star of a beau had even pre-dated Geena's father's divorce.

Yes, she knew, she could definitely write a story based on her father.

When Rob arrived, Geena was laughing. She launched herself onto the porch and into his arms.

"Well, there you are," he murmured into her ear. "You've been so down since you've been home, I was starting to wonder what was up."

When Geena next saw the sidewalk square bearing her name, it was intact, same as always. It had not magically healed itself. Geena's perspective had simply changed. Her outlook had brightened.

Suddenly, nothing about love seemed breakable.

***

Yes, there are two possibilities. Really, though, there is beauty in either theory—if we believe the literal version, that ghosts exist in Ruby's Place, we can take comfort in the idea that death is never the end. That maybe, someday, we might meet our own missed loved ones. We might also get to become a face in the window ourselves. Our legacy continuing on, Christmas after Christmas.

But if we subscribe to the theory that the story is a metaphor, then we can take pleasure in knowing that inside each of us is a Ruby's Place—a space we can all journey to, where we find the ghosts of our own past. We can take pleasure in the sight of bright red cardinals against cold December skies, knowing they are simply a symbol of the bright happy memories that remain once the bad has blurred into a smudgy, gray, wintry background devoid of any detail. (Isn't that truly the way of memories? We hang on to what was happy and forget the bad? Or—isn't it what we strive to do, anyway?)

Ghosts, we would most assuredly say (if we are, in fact, believers of the metaphorical version of this story), are nothing more than memories come to life. And Christmas is the force that pushes us through the door, into the space inside us all, where we keep the past—just as Angela herself once burst through the door of the long-closed Ruby's Place. It is Christmas that allows our memories to become so vibrant, to feel so close.

In the end, the tale of Ruby's Place emerges as a Christmas gift; it is *your* Christmas gift. Meant for you to unwrap, to play with and modify and decorate in a way which makes your own heart sing.

One Last Juicy Tidbit

Gossip continued to swirl, like it always had in Sullivan. "If light bulbs could run on rumors…" after all.

According to Susan Fitzweather at the Senior Center and Kimberly Tan at the florist shop and even Kelly, the lone employee at The Page Turner, just before New Year's, Angela was out running errands—grocery shopping, most agree, that's what she was up to—when she happened to see something strange out there by the high school. A lone figure running the track. Which seemed a little odd, since the kids were still out of school for the holiday. Who came to school by themselves, when they didn't have to?

Angela was still thinking about Christmas, and the lovely surprise of finding out she had been remembered fondly by an old love. She was thinking about all the Christmases that had come before—and Gail, too. Chris had brought it all back. How strong her memories suddenly were! They draped warmly across her shoulders.

She drove her car into the parking lot and walked up to the metal bleachers. She took a seat midway up the stands, pulling her collar up and an old brown hat down to protect her from the cold wind.

She watched the woman run, the decades that had passed feeling as close as yesterday.

The woman running caught sight of Angela and waved. Walked straight to those bleachers.

"Hey, sis," she greeted, still panting from her run.

That's what the gossipers all say, anyway.

Only some believe it.

So it goes with belief.

Come Back to Ruby's Place

Find out how it all started with the original short tale
Christmas at Ruby's

Rob and Geena's love story takes the starring role in
I Remember You

Come Back to Ruby's Place

The speakeasy days come back to Sullivan in
Sentimental Journey

The entire collection is also available as an ebook:
The Ruby's Place Christmas Collection

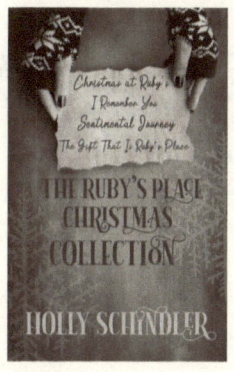

Holly Schindler

Holly Schindler is an award-winning and critically acclaimed author of books for readers of all ages. She firmly believes nothing is quite as magical as a good story or an exciting new "what-if." She is currently chasing down another "what-if" as she writes her next book. She also loves hearing from readers. If you'd like to get in touch or learn more about Schindler's available releases, please visit:

HollySchindler.com